Without God I wouldn't be the person I am

Without my family I wouldn't know love

Without readers I wouldn't be able to live my dream

This book is a work of fiction. All names, characters, locations, and incidents are products of the authors' imaginations. Any resemblance to actual persons, things, living or dead, locales, or events is entirely coincidental.

Edited by Roxanne Herman
Proofread by Magnolia Author Services
Cover by Timeless Designs

Instant HEAT

One night.

One bet.

And now my world is turned upside down.

Apparently, you're not supposed to fall for the rebound guy.

Guess I didn't get the memo, because the first man I jump into bed with happens to be the one who sparks a flame inside my heart.

With his rakish charm and Irish accent, he steals my sanity and inhibitions.

It's not long before I'm dreaming of something more than a quick fling.

The problem?

Griffin Gallagher happens to be the one man my brother despises.

1

RAELYN

"Shots. We need shots."

"Yes!"

My gaze flitted between my two best friends. "And why exactly do we need shots?"

"How else are you going to work up the nerve to pick up a guy tonight?" Lacy flicked her blonde hair over her shoulder and gave me a look that said '*well, duh.*' Next to her, Briana nodded furiously, clearly agreeing. I looked down at my t-shirt and jeans. Not only was I not in the mood to bat my eyelashes at a man, I wasn't dressed for it either. And to be completely honest, the situation with my ex-boyfriend had put me off men for a while.

A long, long while.

Sensing exactly where my mind had gone, Lacy reached over and squeezed my hand. "Come on, Rae, it's been months."

Nine months to be exact. But who was counting? A half-smile that I knew looked as forced as it felt tugged at my lips. "I know, it's just—"

Before the words had time to form, Briana cut in, "No, Rae!" She waved her index finger from side to side. "No more excuses. We know this thing with Rob messed you up, but it's time to take control of your life."

Chewing on the inside of my cheek to keep my smile from spreading, I tried to keep my face straight when I asked, "And I need a man to do that?"

My friend's brows drew together, and she looked a bit annoyed. "No, silly. You need a man to give you a few toe-curling orgasms until you say: *Rob who?*"

"Yes! What she said," Lacy exclaimed.

"Of course," I nodded slowly, "and this obsession you guys have with my sex life is totally normal, right?"

It all started three months ago when the two of them decided—without even talking to me about it—that I needed to get laid. They've made it their sole mission in life to set me up on as many blind dates as they possibly could.

Not that I actually went on any.

I caught on to their shenanigans pretty early on, and would go along with whatever excuse they cooked up to get me to the bar or restaurant only to leave almost immediately.

Still, they didn't stop.

"Rae," Briana's voice drew my attention. "We are worried about you." She leaned forward; her face deadly serious. "You know," she said with her lips pressed together as if she was about to divulge some secret. "Use it or lose it."

Laughter bubbled from the pit of my stomach and didn't stop coming until tears slid down my cheeks, and my ribs ached. "Are you serious right now?" I managed while I tried to catch my breath.

"She has a point," Lacy added, her face solemn. "What if you forget how to do it."

"Oh my goodness." I shook my head in disbelief. "How much have the two of you had to drink?" My narrowed gaze flicked from one to the other. "I'm positive that I will not forget how to have sex."

Briana's slender shoulder rose and fell in a small shrug. "Only one way to find out." The competitive side of me stood up and took notice of the hint of challenge in her voice. "I'll bet you fifty bucks that you can't pick up a guy and leave with him."

"Oooooh, I want in on this." Lacy smacked her palm against the surface of the table.

"You have lost your damn minds."

Sitting up a bit straighter, Brie smiled sweetly before she said, "Okay, what about this: if you manage to leave with a guy tonight, we'll stop setting you up." The smug look on both their faces had me saying, *"You're on,"* before my brain had time to comprehend this was probably a bad idea.

"Let's make this interesting." Lacy tapped a perfectly manicured finger against her chin. "Brie and I choose the guy." When I tilted my head and eyed her suspiciously, she added, "Oh come on, you know we actually want you to get laid. Besides, our douche-meter is a little more accurate than yours."

Ouch, that stung. She wasn't wrong, though. Brie and Lacy had hated Rob from the get-go. They'd said he'd been too smooth, but I'd been too smitten to listen.

"That guy!" Briana jumped to her feet and not-so-subtly pointed toward someone.

Being as short as I was, I had no hope of spotting whoever she was pointing at from my perch. Pushing out of my seat, I followed her gaze and index finger and almost choked. "Oh hell, no! Are you freaking crazy?" I shook my head vehemently. Somewhere out there, there was a woman who thought the pot-bellied, bald-headed look was sexy as all hell. That woman wasn't me though.

Brie pressed her hands to her belly and let out a squeal of laughter. The sheer force of it doubling her over on the spot. Narrowing my eyes, I shot daggers at the top of her head until she straightened and I could shoot them at her face.

"What?" she asked, her voice all sweet and dripping with innocence. My gaze narrowed even further. "At least you won't have to worry about him spending more time in the bathroom than you."

Another dig at Rob brought with it another bout of laughter. And this time I couldn't help but join in. Rob Sinclair took the whole millennium man thing to an entirely different level. He had more moisturizers and face scrubs for his morning routine than Lacy, Brie, and me combined.

And don't even get me started on the mini straightener he had with him almost all the time.

"Him!"

Wiping the happy tears from my eyes, I turned to face Lacy who was transfixed on someone. She wrapped her arm around my shoulders and urged me to face the bar. Brows pulled together in confusion, I asked, "What am I looking for?"

"Dark jeans, black shirt."

I scanned the patrons until I found one matching her very vague description. All I saw was a guy hunched over his beer. Well, to be specific, I saw a dark head bent over and broad, really broad, shoulders that tapered down to a narrow waist.

My focus shifted back to Lacey. "For all I know he might look like that guy," my chin jerked in Mr. Pot-belly's direction, "but with more hair."

Lacey shook her head. "Trust me, he's freaking hot. I thought he was checking me out but his eyes have been on you, Rae. I'm pretty sure you'll only have to smile prettily, and he'll be eating out of your hand."

My gaze skittered back to the bar. Did I want that? To walk up to a stranger and proposition them for a night of hot sex? Not that I had anything against women who did exactly that. I actually thought they were pretty badass.

I was not badass. In fact, considering I'd never picked up a guy before, I'd say I was pretty chicken-shit.

Nibbling on my lip, I eyed Lacy and Brie. "Uhm—"

Both their heads started shaking at the same time, but it was Lacy who spoke. "No way! You're not backing out!" She cupped my shoulders and stooped to look me in the eye. "You're going to walk up to that hunk of a man, and you are going to flirt your ass off until he offers to take you for a ride."

My eyebrow quirked. "Just like that, huh?"

"Yes." She nodded.

Because I wasn't expecting it, she scared the crap out of me when she started fiddling with my ponytail. Annoyed, I swatted her hand away. "The hell?" But she was too determined to see her mission to manhandle—or was that womanhandle?—me through. Abandoning my hair, she smoothed her hands over my shoulders and then lifted my boobs.

Yes, to my complete and utter horror and shame, my friend 'fluffed' the girls. I was ready to die while Brie looked like she was having a seizure. A laughter-induced seizure.

Why was I friends with them again?

Smacking Lacy's hand away, I pinned her with a stare. "Stoppit! I'm going, okay?"

Lacy grinned and folded her arms in front of her. Brie made weird snort noises that had me wondering if we might need an ambulance.

"I thought you said you were going?" Lacy challenged me.

Scrunching up my nose, I tried my best to look intimidating. "I hate you."

Lacy snorted. "Oh please, bish, you love us." She waggled her brows. "And tomorrow morning you'll love us even more."

"I highly doubt that," I muttered under my breath as I turned and headed toward the bar.

2

GRIFFIN

Bloody hell.

Blonde, long legs, curvy hips, and an ample chest. A very ample chest where I could easily rest me head.

Exactly what I needed tonight.

Or so I thought.

The moment the blonde bombshell moved aside, I caught sight of a petite little thing laughing next to her. And for a fraction of a second, time stood completely still. The gentle back and forth of her ponytail as she shook her head, hypnotized me. The black jeans and white t-shirt that might as well have been painted on to her, had me mind running in a million different directions.

But it was her smile that held me captive.

It looked genuine and carefree, it made me want to smile with her. Shaking me head, I focused me frown on the beer in front of me. From the moment I could listen, me da had sprouted tales of the first time he'd seen me ma.

Talked about time standing still and his world shifting into place all in the space of a breath. I'd listened and smiled even though I'd thought it was the biggest load of shite.

But this feeling inside me chest... No, it was definitely just a lack of sex messing with me brain. The body could only take so much self-love until it all felt rather robotic and unsatisfying.

In me defense, the last couple of months had been rough at best. I'd spent a lot of time questioning the unfairness of life and whether I still wanted to do a job I was born to do. So sinking into a warm, willing body hadn't been at the top of the list.

As if under some kind of spell, me head swiveled to seek out the brunette again. Only, she was gone. I'd laid eyes on her just a few minutes ago, so the disappointment that drew me brows together was as strange as it was unwelcome.

"I haven't seen you here before."

I turned me attention to the sweet-sounding voice beside me. Almost immediately, me teeth found the flesh of me cheek to keep me twitching lips from spreading into a smile. Up close, the brunette looked even more beautiful.

Me heart stuttered at the sight of her. Slicking me tongue over me teeth, I grinned at her. "Observant. 'Tis me first time."

A deep blush stole her cheeks and instantly highjacked me thoughts. In me mind, I could already see her skin turning that particular shade under very different circumstances.

On top of me.

Under me.

What sounds would she make? Would she still sound so achingly sweet when she—

"No way." Her voice sliced through the lust-fog covering me brain. I blinked once and her pretty face came back into view. The biggest blue eyes I'd ever seen stared at me. Thick black lashes framing them like a piece of art. *Shite!* Apparently, the lack of sex was turning me into some sort of poet now. "You have an accent."

"Aye, that I do."

That smile that stole me attention from across the room was back. Man, it was gorgeous. *She* was gorgeous. Me goddess rested her elbow on the bar and cradled her face in her palm. A tiny frown pulled her brows together. Her gaze contemplative as it steadily moved down the length of me.

When her eyes met mine, the tip of her tongue slid along her bottom lip. "I'm Raelyn," she offered her free hand. "Everyone just calls me Rae."

A lazy smile lifted me lips. I took the offered hand—
mine almost swallowing hers whole—and squeezed.
"Griffin."

The instant the touch registered, she sucked in a breath,
her gaze darting to our joined hands. I knew then she
felt it too. A zip of electricity—that had nothing to do
with the two beers I'd had—rushed through me veins,
kicking me heart into gear.

Images of her, of us, flashed in me mind one after the
other.

The two of us tangled in me sheets. Walking on the
beach. Her head thrown back in laughter at something
I said. Those big blue eyes shining bright as she leaned
in to kiss me.

What the hell?

I blinked again. Our connected hands the first thing I
saw when me vision shifted from blurry to focused.
This overwhelming need pulsed through me veins to
use the hand tucked inside mine as a lever; yank her
forward and cover those enticing lips with me own.
To kiss her long and hard until me taste was the only
one she knew.

Swallowing, I carefully pulled me hand from hers,
fingers furiously brushing over me palm to get rid of
the sensation burning into me skin.

"Can I get you anything to drink?"

With her brows still knitted together, she looked between me face and her hand like she couldn't decide where to pin her focus. After a few more rounds of ping pong, our eyes finally locked. Her frown still firmly in place as she shook her head. The action was so subtle if I hadn't been watching her so carefully, I would've missed it.

Rae blew out a breath, her lips stretching into a smile a second later. "I've got it." Then she twisted in her seat and signaled the bartender. I was still staring at her like an idiot when she cheerily ordered, "Two shots of Sambuca and a beer, please?"

I didn't care for the taste of Sambuca but I probably would have swallowed down anything this woman offered me. So when the bartender returned with her drink order, I steeled myself for the sharp taste of the liquor, already preparing to knock back the rest of me beer to mask it.

Completely unnecessary.

The moment the two glasses were placed in front of her, she knocked them back and wiped her mouth with the back of her hand. Without taking too much of a breath, she reached for her beer and took two big swigs of it before setting it down on the counter with a loud *thunk*.

I was intrigued.

Either this woman was a party animal or working up the nerve to do something.

She angled her head me way, I was a little surprised to see a hint of uncertainty shine behind her eyes. Her nostrils flared with the deep drag of air she took to her lungs and I did me best not to stare at her chest rising and falling with the action.

"Here's the deal," Rae said. "My friends and I have a bet."

Me brow arched. "This bet wouldn't happen to have anything to do with me?"

Deep crimson stained her cheeks as she nodded and looked past me to where I presumed her friends sat. The uncertainty I'd seen in her eyes now evident on her face too. This stunning woman seemed so sure of herself a few moments ago. What changed in the space of a few minutes?

I was about to ask when she blurted out, "Both of them have money on the fact that I am unable to pick up a guy at a bar... or anywhere else for that matter."

All I could do was stare. Not because of what she said. No, I had a hard time believing that she couldn't pick up a guy. Hell, I was sure men followed her around like puppy dogs with their tongues hanging out.

She must've thought me silence meant something it didn't. A small chuckle left her lips just as she mumbled, "This is stupid." Snatching her beer from the counter, she slipped off her stool and started walking away.

Yeah, I was not having it.

Reaching out, I curled me fingers around her arm and almost swore at how soft her skin felt beneath me touch. The hairs on me neck lifted as electricity zipped up and down me spine. How in the hell could a simple touch have this effect?

Concentrating hard on the woman before me and not the sensations wreaking havoc inside of me, I pushed off the stool too. Once I'd straightened to me full height, Rae looked even more petite. This profound feeling of wrapping her up in me arms and keeping her safe slammed into me chest with so much force, it stole the breath right out of me lungs.

"Don't run away," I said. Big unguarded eyes lifted to meet mine. "Tell me about this bet."

She studied me for long agonizing seconds. "I just did."

"No." I shook me head. "You said there was a bet." I leaned in a bit closer. "But you never told me how I fit." Me voice dropped low. "Do you want to pick me up, Rae?"

"I…" Her throat slowly moved with the swallow she worked down. Her eyes flicking to where I was still holding onto her. For a flicker of a second, I thought she was going to pull away and walk off.

But then I saw determination light up her features. Rae pulled her shoulders back, lifted her chin and looked me dead in the eye. "Yes, I do." Even as she said the words, her cheeks turned bright red.

I wanted to kiss her. Shite, I'd never wanted to kiss anyone as desperately as I wanted to kiss Rae in that moment. Every cell in me body vibrated with the need to surge forward and claim her mouth so thoroughly she forgot anyone before me.

Me grin spread slow and wide as me free hand came up to take the beer in her hand. Without taking me eyes off her, I placed it on the bar behind me. "Right, how do you want to do this?"

Deep lines formed on her forehead. "What?"

"Do you want to just walk out of here?" I let go of her arm to tuck two fingers beneath her chin. "Or we could give them a show… leave them a little speechless?"

Her breath caught in her throat. "I like option two."

She'd barely spoken the words before I stooped and pressed me lips to hers. In that moment there was no space for rational thinking, no time to be a gentleman. The only thing that mattered was the feel of her mouth on mine.

I had to suppress the groan that wanted to rumble free. Her lips were even softer and tastier than I'd imagined and the way she was kissing me right back all but knocked me on me arse.

Licking at the seem of her mouth, I slid me palms around her delicate neck. Me thumbs pushing against her chin keeping her face at the perfect angle. Hot and wet, me tongue eagerly dipped inside.

I hissed out a breath when Rae's hands came to me waist, fingers digging into me sides. The warmth of her touch searing me skin through the material of me shirt. I wanted more. Needed more.

Tilting her head to the side, I deepened the kiss, earning me a sexy little moan that rolled over me skin before hitting me straight in the groin. Still, I needed more. More tasting. More teasing. More Rae.

I took a step forward making sure there wasn't even space for a breath between us. Me ego not the only thing growing when she gasped at what she felt pressed against her.

The kiss deepened even more. Her fingers dug in harder. I wanted to strip her right where we were standing and have me wicked way with her.

Until someone cleared their throat very loudly.

I had no bloody idea how the hell I managed to pull me mouth from Rae's. And when she stared at me with those big eyes and her bottom lip sucked into her mouth, all I could think about was sucking that lip into *me mouth*.

"Wow." Her voice sounded breathless and sexy. So damn sexy. "That was the last thing I expected when I walked over."

Me gaze dropped to her just-kissed lips before slowly lifting to meet hers again. "It's the *only* thing I've wanted to do since laying eyes on you." Under normal circumstances I'd have a few more drinks with the girl, get to know her a little before dragging her off to me bed. With Rae, though, I had this overwhelming need to be alone with her.

Which is exactly why I leaned forward and whispered next to her ear, "You want to get out of here now?"

Her eyes focused somewhere over me shoulder for a beat before she turned her baby blues on me again. It wasn't hard to see that she was trying to work out if she really wanted to leave with me or not. I wasn't going to push, as desperately as I needed to have her all to myself, I needed her to want that too.

We were still standing so close her chest grazed mine when she sucked in an audible breath right before she whispered, "Okay."

That was all I needed to hear. After throwing a few bills next to our discarded beers, I wrapped me fingers around hers and started for the exit. It took me a few strides to realize that for every step I took Rae had to take three just to keep up.

For the entire walk from the bar to the parking lot, Rae's taste lingered on me lips, only making me crave her more. So much so, instead of opening the door for her, I pressed her up against the side of me truck and assaulted her mouth again.

Without missing a beat, we picked up exactly where we left off inside the bar. Tongues slipping and sliding. Tasting. Devouring.

More. More. More.

The word echoed in me brain, vibrated through me veins. I stepped forward, Rae's knee almost immediately sliding up me thigh. Me hand dropped to her hip, the pad of me thumb digging into the soft skin just below her hipbone.

She made a noise. Something between a sigh and a moan. And then went ahead and stole me sanity when she rubbed against me. I'd lost all control over me body when me hips rocked forward.

Hard seeking soft.

Somewhere in the very back of me mind, the thought that I, a grown arse man, was dryhumping a woman against the side of me truck registered. Shite, when did I turn into a horny teenager? Surely, I could keep it in me pants for ten more minutes? Again, I tore me mouth from hers with difficulty. Grinning, I reached for the handle beside her. "You'd better get in before we give these people a show they didn't pay for."

Dark navy eyes peered up at me from beneath even darker lashes, her mouth lifting into a smile. Me heart stuttered right before it slammed against me ribs at the speed of light.

Somehow, I just knew that smile was going to be the death of me.

Rae rolled her lip over her teeth, gaze trained on me mouth. "No," I croaked out. "Get in."

The most adorable little laugh bubbled over her lips before she hopped into the passenger side. I quickly closed the door and rounded the truck even faster. Not even a second later the engine rumbled to life, tires screeching as I pressed me foot to the gas.

Eight minutes later, I pulled into me driveway and cut the engine.

Both Rae and I turned to face each other at the same time. Electricity zipping and zapping in the small space of the cab as we simply stared at each other for long, hot seconds. When her tongue darted over her lips, the band that held me sanity together snapped.

Me hand shot out, fingers hooking behind her neck. With one sharp tug I pulled her face to mine and closed me mouth over hers.

Kissing this woman was like nothing I'd ever experienced. Every stroke of her tongue touching a part of me I had no idea existed. A dormant part that only she had the ability to rouse. Again, me da's words rang through me mind. Sharp and loud.

I pushed it away just as fast.

Focusing on the woman driving me crazy, I pulled at her shirt until I could reach beneath the cotton. An unholy sound hissed past me lips at that first touch. The feel of her soft skin beneath me fingertips had me suffering a sensory overload.

Wanting to touch more of her, I dragged me palm higher until I could fill it with her breast. I groaned. She sighed. We needed more space. I wanted to see her spread out on the floor or the bed. I didn't care where I just knew I needed more room to explore every inch of her body.

"Inside," I managed to croak out around the kiss.

"Yes," she agreed breathily. However, neither one of us made a move to get out of the truck. Instead, our kisses turned more urgent. More hungry. More frantic. Rae dragged her hand down me chest before brushing it over the front of me jeans. I jumped against her exploring fingers and almost lost it.

"Shite, wait." Never before had I jumped out of the truck so fast. I swear, I reached the passenger side in four steps. Just as I opened the door a tiny fist curled into me shirt and yanked me forward. Rae's lips and hands were everywhere.

"The house is just a few feet away, *acushla*." She
wasn't listening, or she was just ignoring me. Either
way, she wasn't stopping and the more she explored
with her mouth and hands the less I could resist.
Left with no other choice, I scooped her up and after
kicking the door shut, I started walking toward the
house. With Rae kissing and nipping at me neck and
ear, something as simple as walking became near
impossible.

Even with all me attention focused on it, I still fumbled
with the key and the door. When we finally made it
inside after way too many attempts, I all but ran
through the house to get to the bedroom. Sure, pressing
her up against the door would've been easier and faster
but I wasn't lying when I said I wanted this woman
sprawled out beneath me where I could take me sweet
time.

Stopping at the foot end of the bed, I reached up and
freed Rae's hair from the band that held it together.
Immediately dragging me fingers from root to tip,
marveling in the silky feel of her strands brushing
against me knuckles.

I'd held out as long as I possibly could—Shite, I didn't
even know how I made it this *long*—and now the need
to have her was almost as desperate as me need to
breathe. Setting her on the bed, I gripped me tee and

pulled it over me head. I wasn't even remotely prepared for the feel of her lips on me naked skin. I hissed out a breath through clenched teethed, fighting hard against the urge to close me eyes. So much… feeling. I didn't know what to do with it all. This was just supposed to be a hookup, wasn't it?

So why did it feel like so much more?

Rae's slow torture continued when her lips moved from me chest all the way down to the waistband of me jeans. As much as I would've liked for her to go lower still, I knew having her mouth on me wasn't the best idea.

One touch and I'd bloody explode.

Pushing me fingers into her hair, I dropped me face to hers for another one of those soul-searing kisses while I coaxed her onto her back. Me hand found the hem of her shirt and swiftly pulled it over her head before getting to work on her jeans.

I swallowed roughly at the sight of her in nothing but pale-yellow underwear. Hungrily raking me gaze up and down the length of her, I was torn between just looking and ripping the satin from her body so I could properly take me fill.

In the end, Rae took the decision from me when she sat up and unclasped the bra before flinging it across the room. Then she tortured me some more by slowly wiggling out of her panties and tossing them aside.

"You're beautiful, Rae."

A blush started at her chest and steadily crawled up her neck before settling on her cheeks. Her eyes shut for a brief moment and when she opened them again, the fire burning behind her irises turned me blood hot. Digging her teeth into her bottom lip, she leaned back onto her elbows.

"And you're completely overdressed," she purred.

I had to bite me lip to stop myself from devouring this gorgeous creature beneath me. Mauling and pawing at her like a beast was only going to have it over before it even began. Repeating *that* sentence in me head, I stripped out of the rest of me clothes and slowly came down over her.

I kissed her again, taking me time. Nipping and sucking on her skin as I made me way down her body. Her moans became louder, needier, the lower I moved. And when me teeth found her hipbone, the sounds bouncing off the walls reached an all-time high. Smiling against her skin, I moved lower still. Once I had that first taste of her though, I knew I wanted more. Me fingers dug into her skin. Her moans grew louder. Her hips restless.

It wasn't all that long before a satisfied sigh blew over her lips. Crawling up her body, I took her mouth in another hot kiss before I finally, *finally*, got to lose myself in the warmth of her.

"You feel amazing," was the only coherent thought I could form before nothing but grunts and groans came out where words were supposed to be. Everything around me—except the woman beneath me—disappeared, and I was lost to need and desperation. I didn't even know how long it was before I breathlessly collapsed onto the mattress beside her. Lazily Rae turned her head to face me, the satisfied look on her beautiful face bringing a smile to me lips.

"Guess I can pick up a guy after all."

The laugh that rumbled its way from inside me couldn't be helped. Gathering her close, I bit me tongue before I said something crazy like, *'As long as I'm the only guy you pick up.'*

Even when I drifted off to sleep with Rae snuggled up against me that thought never left.

3

RAELYN

A soft breeze blew over my cheek causing me to pop one eye open. I couldn't help but smile when I saw where it came from. *Griffin*. I shut my eye before quickly opening both this time. *Yep, he's still here.* Pushing onto my elbow, I admired the man who had rocked my world—multiple times—a few hours ago. His thick black hair thoroughly disheveled, the whiskers peppering his jaw a few shades darker already. I bit my lip to keep myself from moaning at the memory of how good it felt when his scruff scraped along my skin. How his big hands roamed all over my body. The way he kissed and how his gaze had the ability to caress my skin.

Or that damn accent.

Did he even know it got thicker in the throes of passion? At some point, it'd sounded like the man had been making reverent promises to me in his mother tongue.

Oh, what a tongue.

Shaking my head, I slipped from the bed and went in search of my clothes. As I donned item after item, I kept my gaze on Griffin's sleeping form. This was supposed to be a one-night-stand, but I already felt some strange connection to this man. The thought of never seeing him again didn't sit quite right with me. Which was of course utterly stupid.

Just as I closed the snap of my jeans my phone vibrated from my back pocket. My entire body jerked, and it took all the effort I could muster not to curse out loud and accidentally wake the Irish sex god.

Clutching my chest, I pulled out my phone. My brother's name flashed in big bold letters. Scrunching up my nose, I sent him to voicemail before shoving the phone back into my pocket. But not before seeing seven missed calls.

Seven.

Yeah, Thatcher was definitely taking his role as the protective big brother way too seriously. It wasn't like I didn't appreciate him looking out for me. Sometimes it was just a bit too much.

He'd turned into a helicopter mom hellbent on keeping me from making silly mistakes... again. With a sharp shake of my head, I tip-toed to the bed. Griffin was still fast asleep.

Crawling in next to him was so damn tempting, but I couldn't. Because as Thatcher liked to remind me, I had a tendency to fall fast and hard. It happened with Rob and every boyfriend I'd had before him too.

Still staring at the beautiful man sprawled on the bed, I brought my hand up and pressed my palm between my breasts. *This feels different, though.*

No! Just because the man kissed like he was put on this earth to do only that or because he could deliver orgasms like it was his job, didn't mean whatever the heck I was feeling was different.

It was a sex high. Yes, that's it. My emotions were running high because my hormones needed time to stabilize. Feeling much better now that I had an explanation for the butterflies in my belly and the steady current rolling over my skin, I gave Griffin one more longing look before slowly walking backward out of the room.

Since I'd been too preoccupied when we arrived, I only now noticed whose house this was. Donald and Leah Kruger. After the Fire Chief retired almost two years ago, he and his wife had decided to spend their time traveling around the world.

As far as I knew, they never sold their house because they always made their way back to West Kirksin for the holidays. They also never had kids. So how the heck did they know an Irishman from who-knew-where?

My gaze skittered over the gray couch covered with yellow and lime green scatter cushions before landing on a stack of boxes next to the door. Unable to resist, I moved closer. They hadn't even been opened yet. When exactly did Griffin blow into town and from where? The man was all kinds of intriguing and I had this overwhelming feeling that I needed to know more. Without too much overthinking, I marched to the kitchen and grabbed the notepad stuck against the fridge door.

***

"Where the hell have you been?"

I startled at the sound of Thatch's angry voice. Both hands flew to my chest, pressing hard against my racing heart. Spinning on my heel, I leveled the idiot with a stare. "What the hell?"

I was positive if an intruder walked in right this second, they'd turn and run in the opposite direction. My asshat brother was *that* scary looking with his legs spread wide and his bulging biceps crossed over an even bigger chest.

To me, he just looked ridiculous.

"I was worried sick, Rae. You didn't answer any of my calls."

He sounded so much like our mother in that moment, I almost laughed. Almost. Our parents died in a robbery gone wrong six years ago. Thatch had barely graduated while I was still making my way through school.

The responsibility of being a parent was thrown onto him before he'd even had time to live his life. He'd taken it in his stride. Never complaining. I actually kind of got the idea he'd liked the feeling of being needed.

It was why I still hadn't moved out of the house our parents had left us.

"I was busy, okay?" I pushed past the six-foot-four wall in my way and padded to the kitchen where I grabbed a bottle of orange juice from the fridge. As I gulped down the zesty liquid, I heard my brother enter.

"Busy with what?" he practically growled.

I closed my eyes and took a deep breath. He was just worried about me, I knew this. If our situations had been reversed, I'd probably do the same thing. But they weren't, and right now, Thatch was smothering me with his over-protectiveness.

Sucking in a steadying breath, I twisted the cap back onto the bottle and slowly turned to face my brother. "It's been nine months, Thatch. I'd really need to get some normalcy back into my life."

The features that looked so much like my own softened as he pushed off the frame and approached me. "I worry about you." I heard the concern in his voice, so when he pulled me in for a hug, I went willingly. "You had a good night, then?" he asked into my hair.

My lips lifted into a smile out of their own volition, "The best."

After he released me, Thatcher snatched the orange juice from my hand, unscrewed the cap and swallowed down what was left of it. After wiping his mouth with the back of his hand, he bared his teeth in a wide grin. Seeing him smile was such a rare occurrence, I couldn't help but do the same.

"Were you out with a boy?" he asked, waggling his brows.

A very unladylike snort-laugh sounded from the back of my throat before I planted my fists on my hips and gave my brother a pointed stare, "I am twenty-two years old, I do not go out with *boys*, thank you very much."

Thatcher practically howled with laughter while I did my best not to tell him exactly how much of a man Griffin was. I might've been wrong, but I didn't think my brother would want to hear about his little sister's sexpeditions.

I let out a yelp when Thatch hooked his ginormous arm around my neck and rubbed his knuckles against my scalp. No matter how hard I pushed at him, he didn't budge. He only let go of me went he was satisfied that my hair was thoroughly mussed.

Idiot.

"Well, now that the prodigal daughter has returned, I can finally get some shut-eye." My brother very dramatically announced. He pulled a face of disgust before he said, "The new guy starts in the morning."

I felt bad for Thatch; he'd worked his butt off only to get passed up for a promotion yet again. For as long as I could remember my brother had wanted to be a firefighter; he was good at it. But he was also a bit of a hothead; he acted without thinking things through and that had landed him in trouble more than once.

It also meant that he wasn't a very strong candidate when a new position became available. Even though I understood the reasoning, I still hated this for my brother. But if I told him one more time how sorry I was about it all, he'd flip his lid. Instead, I placed my hand on his forearm and squeezed gently. "Your time will come. Promise."

He eyed me for a long moment. "Yeah, maybe you're right."

"Of course I am."

Thatch draped his arm over my shoulder as we walked out of the kitchen together. "No more late nights with *boys*, yeah?"

I brought my hand up and patted his chest. "No more late nights with boys." Shrugging out from under his arm, I paused just inside my bedroom door. "Now, strong virile men… that's an entirely different story." My brother made a face. I threw my head back and laughed right before shutting my door and resting my forehead against the wood.

Yeah, I definitely couldn't promise my brother there wouldn't be anymore late nights with a certain dark-haired Irishman.

4

GRIFFIN

What the hell?

Sitting up, I aimed me frown at the empty space next to me. Where a warm, sexy body should have been were nothing but cold sheets. No strewn about clothes on the floor when I looked there too.

I wasn't being cocky, but I could honestly say this was the first time a woman had slipped out of me bed in the middle of the night. Usually, I was the one doing the early morning sneaking.

I wasn't quite sure how to feel.

It didn't take long for me to settle on disappointed. Because as much as I was hoping to love on Rae's body again, I wanted to sit and have breakfast with her. Learn more about her. Get her number, so I could take her out on a proper date.

She intrigued me. A lot.

With a heavy sigh, I closed me eyes and leaned back against the headboard. Images of Rae dancing behind me lids almost immediately. The goosebumps popping up when I brushed me fingers over her soft skin. The way her lips parted right before me name rolled off her tongue in a breathless whisper.

I swear, I could still feel her, smell her.

Heaving out a frustrated groan, I scraped a palm over me face. How the hell was I going to find her?

Me phone buzzed obnoxiously from me bedside table, instantly replacing me thoughts of Rae with something else entirely. Something a lot less enticing.

I loved me job, I really did, but I wasn't looking forward to today. At all. Being the new guy anywhere was daunting.

Being the new lieutenant at a fire station, even more so.

I'd known when I'd asked Donald to help me with this position I was going to piss a few people off.

Firehouses were like families and right now, I was the unwanted stepchild.

With a rough swipe of me thumb, I silenced me alarm before climbing out of bed and making me way to the shower. I waited until steam coated the ceiling before stepping under the warm spray.

Hands braced on the tiles in front of me, I hung me head, enjoying the feel of the water rolling down me back. The only thing that would've made this even better was if Rae had been in here with me.

Shite, the wicked things I could've done to her hot little body.

Not the best train of thought to follow since the temperature inside the stall wasn't the only thing rising. I looked down and cocked a brow. "Not happening."

Yanking on the faucet, I shoved it to the coldest setting. Hissing out a breath when the water pelting down on me felt like ice striking me skin. With any luck that would be enough to keep me mind from wondering to Rae long enough to actually clean up and get ready.

It wasn't.

Honestly, I didn't think there existed anything strong enough to make me forget her for even a second. It was crazy as all hell but after one night, she'd gone and burrowed her way under me damn skin.

Maybe this was what me da was referring to all those times he went on and on about the day he met me ma. I hated to even think it but there might've been something to the old man's ramblings after all.

And that thought alone almost had me laughing me arse off. I didn't believe in fate or destiny or whatever fancy word people liked to call it. It was all just a big steaming pile of shite.

And yet... this feeling strumming behind me breastbone begged to differ.

Shaking me head, I tucked me shirt into me pants and stalked toward the kitchen. With every step I took, me mind furiously searching for ways to find me sexy little brunette. Because I *had* to find her.

Once I entered the kitchen, I opened three different cupboards before I found the coffee grounds and then two more when I went in search of the cups. It probably would have been easier if instead of going to a bar, I'd stayed in and familiarized myself with me new sleeping quarters.

But when I'd arrived in town yesterday, I'd felt a restlessness in me bones that led me straight to the nearest bar.

To Rae.

Shite, I was bloody losing it.

Dragging one hand over the back of me neck, I filled me mug with coffee and almost immediately lifted it to me lips. That first taste of caffeine buzzing through me veins like an electric current. I hummed in approval before going back for another taste.

After swallowing down almost half of me black liquid, I set the mug on the counter so I could scavenge the fridge. With me hand on the handle, I paused. Stuck beneath a magnet that looked like a cupcake was a shockingly pink note. The three words and scribbled digits on it making me damn day.

Call me.

Rae

xoxo

I reached into me pocket to retrieve me phone, fully
intending to do just that. As I wrapped me fingers
around the device, it buzzed to life. One look at the
name flashing on the screen and I dropped the thing as
if it had burned me.

Mildred was as much a ma to me as me own, but I
couldn't talk to her right now. Couldn't explain why I
left without even saying goodbye. Me heart squeezed
tightly inside me chest. They didn't deserve this. Not
from me. And especially not with how things were
going with their son, Adam.

We were as close as brothers, him and I. We'd met a
couple of years after I'd first moved to the States.
Funny enough, we'd both been hitting on the same girl
that night. Four years later, I'd been the best man at
their wedding. Two months after that we'd started
training together and eventually, we were stationed at
the same house.

Everything had been good. Great even. Until it wasn't.
And life reminded us how cruel it could be. I'd lost me
best friends in the blink of an eye. And as desperately
as his parents needed me, I needed space even more.
Seeing them day in and day out only reminded me of
how miserably I'd failed when it really mattered.

Shoving me fingers through me hair, I grabbed the
mug from the counter and emptied what was left of the

coffee. Me movements were jerky when I rinsed it under cold water and set it on the dry rack next to the sink.

Appetite lost too, I grabbed me keys from where they were hanging, climbed into me truck, and made the fifteen-minute drive to Station Sixty-Three.

**

Drumming me fingers against the wheel, I stared at the brick building. Station Sixty-Three.

Me house.

With that thought me fingers stilled. Adam at the forefront of me mind yet again. He'd been the best damn lieutenant I'd worked with. So much so when things went horribly south, and I was asked to fill his shoes, I refused.

I didn't just refuse, I quit.

I hadn't even cleared me locker before I made the call to Donald and begged him for a favor. How desperate I'd been to get away from the memories haunting me was evident in how fast I'd accepted the lieutenant position at Sixty-Three.

I didn't want to lead a team, I was perfectly happy just being part of one. Now, here I was leading one I didn't know shite about. I'd bet Adam would be laughing his arse off if he knew.

Yeah, like Adam could feel anything other than hate.
With that somber thought, I shoved at the door and stepped onto the street. The firehouse was already buzzing with the new shift relieving the last one. I grabbed me duffel from the truck, threw it over me shoulder and took a deep breath before I made me way toward the building.

Two men walked past me, nodding a greeting. Judging by their bloodshot eyes, last night must have been a long one. But those kinds of nights were what I lived for. Nothing like running into a burning building while half of the world was still asleep.

The high was like nothing you could ever imagine. Unfortunately, the lows were pretty catastrophic. Not being able to save someone will haunt you for the rest of your life. It will steal your dreams and hijack your sober thoughts.

I stepped onto the sidewalk just as a car came rolling down the street. Me jaw landed somewhere at me feet a few seconds later. Because sitting pretty behind the wheel of the silver Mazda was the gorgeous brunette who'd been in me bed mere hours ago.

Me gaze zeroed in on the license plate, hands furiously patting me pockets in search of me phone. *Shite.* I'd left the thing at home. And I wouldn't be able to get the damn thing until me shift was over—me twenty-four-hour shift.

With Rae's disappearing car me sole focus, I paid no attention to where I was going and almost plowed over a pedestrian. "Ah, shite, sor—"

"Your mama never told you to watch where you're going, asshole?"

What the? Me gaze snapped to the mumbling idiot, the curses I had ready for him dissolving on me tongue the instant I saw he was a fellow fireman. As much as I itched to teach this big dumbass a thing or two about manners, it wasn't going to get me very far.

People who already hated me would just hate me even more and that would make for a very insufficient firehouse.

So, I told me ego to stand down as I held me hand out to Dumbass. "Sorry, man."

He stopped swatting at the wet spot on his shirt, his gaze locked on me outstretched hand. When he finally met me stare, there was nothing but ice in his eyes. "You the new LT?"

Instead of voicing me answer, I gave him a curt nod. Dumbass puffed out his chest and clasped his hands behind his back before he ground out, "Well, you can go ahead and piss off." With that, he spun on his heels and stomped into the building.

Yeah, the next twenty-four hours were sure as shite going to be interesting.

5

RAELYN

"You little hussy."

I was in the middle of placing my purse in my locker when the words reached my ears. Bag still in hand, I turned to face my accuser. Lacy stood with her shoulder propped against the doorframe looking quite pleased with herself.

"You talking to me?" Feigning innocence, I made a show of searching the room before I pointed a finger at myself.

"Pfft," Lacy pushed off the frame and stalked toward me, a small purse dangling from her fingers. "This look familiar?" She asked. "It should. You were in such a hurry to get out of there last night, you forgot it. Good thing you drove to the bar with me, otherwise it'd be your car keys hanging from my pretty little finger."

Damn, I was really hoping I'd left the thing in Griffin's truck. It would have made for a great excuse to show up at his place without an invitation. I had to admit, I was more than a little disappointed that he hadn't texted yet. I knew he was supposed to be the rebound guy, the one to get me out of my funk.

Maybe I was being silly but last night I'd felt more than a physical connection and I wanted to explore that.

"Helllooooo." My friend's annoyed voice and snapping fingers pulled me from whatever hole I'd fallen into.

I blinked a few times until I could focus on her face. "Huh?"

"Oh geez, Rae, you zoned out."

Embarrassment had my cheeks heating up, and I guessed they were red too. I shook my head and scrunched up my nose. "Sorry." Snatching my bag from Lacy's grip, I stuffed it along with the other one into my locker.

"You're going to make me ask, aren't you?"

"I don't know what you're talking about." Barely managing to hold my laugh, I pushed past my friend and headed to the breakroom. I didn't have to look to know Lacy was short on my heels.

Once I busied myself with the makings of coffee, I could feel her eyes burn a hole in my skull. Still, I refused to look at her. Not because I was ashamed, though. Nope, the huge smile that refused to leave my lips since the early hours of the morning would be a dead giveaway of the fantastic time I'd had.

And that would just have Lacy rubbing my nose in the fact that she and Brie had been right all along.

I grabbed the milk along with a yogurt from the fridge and after slowly whitening my coffee, I turned to face my friend. How I managed to keep my composure with her looking at me like she was ready to take my head off, I would never know.

"Would you like some?" I held my coffee mug toward her, and I swear steam came out of her ears.

"What I would like, *Rae*—" She tucked her arms under her huge boobs and impatiently tapped her foot. "—are details."

Apparently, I was feeling incredibly brave because I just poked a ticking time bomb when I took another leisurely sip of my caffeine.

"Oh, come on!" Lacy complained. "This isn't funny anymore."

My smile grew wider when I exchanged my coffee for some yogurt. After two spoonfuls, I took pity on Lacy and motioned for her to join me at the table by the window.

I'd never seen my friend take a seat that fast before.

"Tell me everything." Leaning forward, she rested her arms on the surface in front of her. The excitement rolling off her zapping like a live wire in the space between us.

"It was—" I chewed on the inside of my cheek not only to torture Lacy but to keep myself from over-excitedly spilling all the details. Lacy and Brie had been in my life for as long as I could remember, I loved them about as much as I loved Thatch—some days maybe even a little more.

But as much as they meant to me, I didn't want to share Griffin with either one.

That thought freaked me out more than a little. No man had ever been off limits when it came to my friends. Hell, they'd known I'd slept with Rob minutes after it'd happened.

When Lacy impatiently drummed her fingers on the table, I realized I hadn't finished my sentence.

"—nice," I finally said.

Seeing a grown woman roll her eyes more dramatically than a teenager was something to behold. "Nice? Really, Rae?" She sounded exasperated. "You don't have a better word than *nice*?" I opened my mouth to say something, but she silenced me by stabbing her index finger in the air. "Everyone at the bar saw that bone-melting kiss and from our vantage point, it looked a whole lot better than *nice*."

This time I didn't hide my smile as the memories of that kiss—and the other toe-curling things we'd done—came flooding back. "Fine, it was amazing. *He* was amazing."

"That's more like it."

Laughter bubbled from inside and spilled over my lips. "Yeah, yeah, don't get too excited, I'm not giving you a play by play."

"Aah, you're no fun anymore." Scrunching up her nose, she pursed her lips. The disappointment on her face only made me laugh even more.

"I can tell you that he's Irish and his kisses made my toes curl."

Lacy reached forward and snatched my yogurt from me. "Poor Mr. Bishop is going to be devastated when he hears you're off the market."

Mr. Bishop was one of our oldest residents at Shady Oaks, the care facility for the elderly where Lacy and I worked. I'd never intended on staying on this long when I'd started helping out during the summer of my senior year.

When the time came to go off to college, I simply couldn't bring myself to leave the people who'd taken up such a big space in my heart. And because Thatch never pushed me to go either— Helicopter brother that he is, I fully believe his only reason for not pushing was so he could continue to keep an eye on me—I stayed.

Turning my face to the window, I took in the yard beyond it. Bright yellow rays reached through the branches, illuminating small spots where it kissed the grass. I couldn't hear them, but I just knew the birds were happily singing their morning song.

"One night of hot sex doesn't mean I'm suddenly taken." I gave Lacy a quick glance before returning my gaze to the outside.

"No, but that look on your face means you want to be." There was a short pause and then, "When are you seeing him again."

I pulled my shoulders to my ears before letting them fall. "I don't know. I kinda snuck out this morning."

"What? Why?"

The sigh blowing over my lips was way too heavy for this early in the day. "I don't even know." How could I explain to her, without sounding like I belonged in the cuckoo's nest, that the enormity of what I felt when I woke up next to him was what drove me out of his bed in the first place?

Of course my friend thought it was something else. Reaching across the table, she covered my hand with hers. "Oh sweetie, not all guys are like Rob. He's in a douchewaffle class all by himself." She squeezed my fingers reassuringly.

"Yeah, I know." I chewed on my lip. "I did leave my number though."

"Good," Lacey drawled as she pushed to her feet. "If he knows what's good for him, he'll call… soon."

I got up too and after throwing the yogurt container in the bin and rinsing my mug, Lacy and I headed out. With a quick hug, we went our separate ways. As usual, my first stop of the day was Mr. Bishop's room. "Good morning, Mr. B," I chimed. Walking over to the window, I drew the curtains back allowing the morning sun entry.

"You know," Mr. Bishop said, his voice sounding every bit as shaky as his seventy-four years. "One of these days you're going to call me by my first name. Especially once we're married and all."

My grin was wide as I got his wheelchair from the other side of the room—which was really more of a mini bachelor flat—and rolled it over to his bed.

"Maybe I'm just saving the name-calling for our wedding day." I batted my lashes very dramatically before helping him into his chair.

His bony elderly fingers sought mine out but couldn't quite make it to where I was holding onto his wheelchair. Taking pity on him, I reached over his shoulder and took his hand in mine. "You're very sweet to indulge an old man."

I felt the squeeze I gave his hand all the way to my heart. Mr. Bishop didn't have anyone left. His wife had died two days before her fiftieth birthday and his only son was killed in a bike accident a few years after that.

I understood the pain of losing not one but two people you loved. At least I still had Thatcher. He'd made the passing of our parents… not easier but rather more manageable. I could even imagine all the kinds of messed up I would have been if it hadn't been for my brother.

That was why if Mr. Bishop needed a few jokes to get through his day, I was definitely going to indulge him. Once I brought his chair to a stop in front of the window, I locked the wheels in place before moving to crouch in front of him. Placing my hand on his knee, I told him, "I'll be back with your breakfast in a bit. When you're done eating, I'll take you for a ride through the garden and we'll talk more about this wedding of ours." I pinned him with a stare. "But only if you finish all your food and take your medicine."

His glassy blue eyes sparkled as much as they could and his deeply lined mouth stretched into a shaky smile. "Got it."

I pushed to my feet and grinned right back. "Back soon."

As I headed out of Mr. Bishop's room, my back pocket buzzed. I reached for my cellphone so fast, one would think I was going for a world record. The excitement buzzing in my veins quickly vanished the instant I read the text.

Thatch: *Just met the new guy, he's a dick.*

A . K .   M A C B R I D E

6

GRIFFIN

Hands clasped behind me back, feet spread wide, I stood next to the Fire Chief as he introduced me to Station Sixty-Three. By the looks on their faces, most of them weren't too pleased I was there.

Our Driver Engineer, Thatcher Brooks, the least pleased of them all.

He was also the guy who'd given me that *warm* welcome earlier. When I found out his position at the station, I knew why though. It was common knowledge that a DE advances to Lieutenant, especially one that has been with the station for so long.

So, yeah, I didn't have to be happy about it, but the guy had a valid reason for being ticked off. Hell, that first time Adam got passed over for a promotion he'd ran his fist through the wall much to Angie's dismay. Shite, I had to stop thinking about the past. The trouble was if I wasn't thinking about Adam and everything he'd lost, me mind kept replaying the night with me sexy little brunette. And thinking about Rae and her curves in the middle of a meeting—or anywhere out in the open, for that matter—was only going to embarrass me.

I shoved the thoughts to the back of me mind just in time to hear Chief Abbott say, "I think that covers it." *Bloody hell.* All the mindless thinking had caused me to miss most of what the chief had said. Eyes bouncing from person to person as they busied themselves with their normal routine, I tried and failed to recall the chief's instructions.

This certainly was not the best way to start me first day.

Spinning around, I decided to head up to me office when tension suddenly curled around me spine. I felt compelled to look left and found Thatcher Brooks staring daggers at me from across the room.

Me sympathy with the dickhead only ran so far. He needed to get the hell over himself and focus on keeping the team running smoothly. A mixture of frustration and exasperation vibrated through me body, that little voice at the back of me mind all but yelling that I'd made one hell of a mistake coming here.

I dragged me fingers through me short hair just as the chief's palm connected with me shoulder blade. His softly-lined face filling me vision a second later.

"You've been doing this for a while, Gallagher," he said, "So you know this transition won't be easy." When I nodded, he continued, "I've spoken to your previous Chief and I'm aware of your situation. You have my sympathy, son, but that doesn't mean I'm going to go easy on you. We run a tight ship here at Sixty-Three, and I expect things to be no different than yesterday or the day before."

Squaring me shoulders, I clasped me hands behind me back. "Of course, sir."

"Good." Crooking his fingers over his shoulder, he motioned for someone to join us. "Brooks will give you the quick two-cent tour." With that Chief Abbott stalked off to his office leaving me alone with the one guy who probably wanted me head on a stick.

Before I could even say a word, Thatcher leaned forward and gritted out, "Just because the chief and Donald think so highly of you doesn't make you being here right."

I'd had just about enough of this guy. "Listen, you arse weed, I'm here. I'm staying. So why don't we make this as easy as possible… You stay the hell out of my way, and I'll do the same."

Fury burned bright in his eyes. His nostrils flared. I dug me heels in and balled up me fists; if this dickhead was going to take a swing, best believe I was going to take one back. Thatcher opened his mouth then quickly snapped it shut again.

A small crease formed on his forehead, the only visible proof of how hard he was trying to compose himself.

And when he spoke a moment later, I had no doubt the words were not the ones rolling around in his head.

"You can find your own damn way around."

Me gaze stayed on him as he stomped over to the rig to do his morning checks.

"I wouldn't pay too much attention to his temper tantrum." I turned me attention to the person speaking to me right. "Nathan." He held out a hand, and I took it. "Thatcher is a bit of a hot-head on a normal day."

What was I supposed to say? The only thing I came up with was, "Right."

Nathan chuckled and then started walking away before stopping and motioning over his shoulder, "C'mon, let me show you around."

***

With a heavy sigh, I dropped me bag to the floor and slumped against the door. The last twenty-seven hours had been anything but easy. I'd barely stepped foot into me new office when we'd received a medical call. Anxiety attack and possible overdose.

Things could have gone smoother on the scene, but unfortunately, even the probies were hellbent on showing their disapproval with me new position. I ended up escorting the patient to the hospital alone. And then just to make sure I understood his big FU,

Thatcher drove the rig straight back to the station instead of picking me up.

Leaving me to cover the five miles back to work on foot.

I'd contemplated writing Brooks up. His actions were not only disrespectful but insubordinate too. Thing was, it didn't matter that a piece of paper or a title on a door gave me authority over these men. If I wanted them to listen and respect me, I'd have to earn it. And I sure as shite wasn't going to do that by writing up Brooks.

I could only hope by the time we were faced with running into a burning building together, our crap would be sorted out.

Pushing off the door, I headed for the kitchen and found me phone on the counter where I'd left it. I swiped it to life and immediately wished I hadn't when I saw the text message waiting for me.

Ma Mildred: *I won't pretend my heart isn't breaking because I didn't get to say goodbye. Heath says you need your own space to heal and I can understand that. Just know no matter where you find yourself, you'll always have a home with us. We love you just as much as we love Adam and Zoe. Don't you ever forget that. Good luck at the new station. And be safe.*

Me heart turned over inside me chest. Bringing me hand up, I furiously rubbed at the spot. I'd been a dick to the people who loved me and still I couldn't bring myself to pick up the phone and give them the apology they deserved.

I hung me head in shame. Me ma and da did not raise me this way. With a sigh, I looked up; me eyes instantly landing on the pink note still stuck to the fridge. Walking over, I pulled it off and studied it long and hard.

It took all me willpower not to dial the number scribbled neatly at the bottom of the page. But I knew the moment I heard Rae's voice; I'd want to see her. Even though me day was at its end, hers had just started.

Still staring at the note, me vision became blurry, and a yawn worked its way to the surface. I needed to get some good sleep and then hope like hell Rae wasn't going to be pissed when I called her tonight.

7

GRIFFIN

Me lungs burned with every ragged breath I took.
Smoke blurred me vision. And I felt the heat of the
flames seep through me gear. Or maybe that was just
me mind playing tricks on me.

"Adam!" I yelled.

He'd run inside mere minutes ago—without gear—he
couldn't have gotten far. Unless… No, I couldn't allow
me mind to go there. The fight wasn't over until the
last damn body was dragged out.

"Adam!" I yelled again. Where the hell are you? *The*
flames hiss to me right before a beam tore off the
ceiling with a loud crack and crashed to the floor.
Shite! I grabbed the radio attached to me arm.

"Bosnan, talk to me."

Static followed and me heart sputtered. Again, I
growled into the tiny device. "Bosnan! Report!"

Long agonizing seconds of static followed before his
distorted voice reached me. "It's not good."

More beams broke from the ceiling, furiously smashing
to the ground. Sparks lit up the smoke-filled room.

Panic held me heart in a vice-grip. I needed to find Adam and Angie.

"Don't talk in bloody riddles, man," I barked into the radio. "Whadda mean, it's no good?"

More bloody static. I was about two seconds away from losing me shite completely. "Ericson found Mrs. Carlisle... she... uh... didn't make it."

Shite! No. Not Angie. I ducked into the living room. The same one Adam and I had had a few beers in two nights ago. The same one where Angie had spent her nights reading on the couch while Adam watched sports.

I was about to ask if they were sure when I spotted a familiar body pinned to the floor. Me friend—me brother—lay trapped beneath an angry gleaming beam. When the stench of burning flesh filled me nose, I knew it wasn't me mind playing tricks on me.

Me hands trembled when I gripped the radio yet again. "I found the LT. He's trapped. We're in the living room. Second door to your left. Hurry."

I had no idea where I got the strength to lift the smoldering beam off me friend. Or even how I managed to haul his six-foot-six frame over me shoulder. All I knew one moment we were still inside Adam's burning house and the next I was sitting in a hospital room.

Dangling me hands between me legs, me shoulders slumped, me head hung low. How in the hell was I supposed to tell me friend his wife was gone? I swallowed thickly at the emotion stuck in me throat. Angie had been as good a friend to me as Adam. And now she was gone.

Shite, me heart hurt. It hurt so damn much that even taking a breath was painful. Fighting fires, saving lives… it was me job. And yet, when it really mattered, I couldn't do shite.

"A..angie…"

Me head snapped up. Adam was blinking rapidly, trying to shift his injured body side to side. Bandages stretched from his neck, covering his chest and his left arm. No doubt, he was in a world of hurt.

I squeezed me eyes shut. His pain was about to be ramped up. It wasn't fair. Shite, it wasn't fair. Slowly opening me eyes, I pushed off the couch and approached the bed. The wild look in me friend's eyes sliced straight through me heart.

"Angie?" he asked.

Me throat burned hot; me eyes even hotter. Steadily, I shook me head. "I'm so sorry."

"No!" Adam's voice boomed. Thrashing wildly, he yelled again, "No!

"Adam."

I moved to put me hand on his right shoulder, but he smacked it away. "Don't touch me... I hate you!" he spat. The force of his words pushing me backward as if he'd shoved them into me chest. "You did this!" More verbal shoving. Me legs shook as I took two more steps backward. "It's your fault she's dead."

Gasping for air, I continued moving backward. Picking up me pace until something dug into me back. Loud clattering of metal reached me ears a second later. The sound so shrill, I wanted to cover me ears.

I quickly spun around. A nurse was on her haunches gathering a tray and fallen medication. I would've stopped to help her if the walls weren't closing in on me, if the air I was pulling to me lungs didn't feel like fire burning through me soul.

Faster and faster me feet moved, Adam's accusations shortly on me heels. By the time I stumbled through the hospital doors and the cool night air hit me skin, I knew everything was about to change.

***

"Shite!"

Heart pounding too loud, too fast, I shot up and scrubbed a palm over me sweat covered face.

Me phone chimed to life from its perch on me bedside table. I'd fully intended on ignoring it until I saw me da's name flash on the screen.

With a trembling hand, I reached for it. Once me thumb swiped over the green button, I pressed the device against me ear. "*Dia dhuit.*"

He coughed into me ear before his raspy voice sounded. "*Dia is Muire dhuit.* Did I wake you, son? I know it's late there."

After taking in me dark surroundings, I admitted, "It was time to wake up anyway. Is everything all right, Da?"

"Yes, yes," he reassured me. "Your ma and I were wondering how the move and new job is going?"

Pushing off the bed, I walked to the window. I couldn't see much of anything beyond it, but that didn't matter. "It's…" A defeated sigh pushed past me lips. "I didn't have the best start, to be honest."

Howling wind filtered through the line and I imagined me da walking across the land, wind whipping the gray hairs on top of his head in every which way. I might've lived in the States but Ireland would always be me home and right that second, I missed it.

Or maybe because I'd been reminded how short life was it was me family I was missing.

"Nothing worth doing is ever easy, son."

Closing me eyes, I leaned me forehead against the cold glass. "I know."

"You keep at it and your reward will be just." He paused for a few seconds. "Your ma and I believe in you and you've made us very proud."

"*Go raibh maith agat*, Da." I pulled in a deep drag of air. "How's Ma doing?"

At the other end of the line, me da sighed heavily. "She's ready to spit fire. Thirty-one of her sheep have gone missing and ole Doyle has reported fifteen missing too. Whoever is taking these animals clearly know what they're doing."

I bit the inside of me cheek to keep from chuckling. Ma's sheep were her babies. I was certain she was livid and until she could take it out on the arse who'd stolen her sheep, me poor da was going to get it.

"That's unfortunate, I hope it gets sorted soon." More heavy sighs filtered through the line. "Me too, son." The words had barely left his mouth when I heard me ma calling for him. I knew that tone all too well. "I have to go feed the horses," he said quickly. The line went dead a second later.

I was still standing in front of the window long after me da had hung up. Staring into the darkness, me thoughts consumed with nothing and everything at the same time. It was this feeling gnawing at me bones that'd driven me to the bar a couple of nights ago.

Drink wouldn't take it away but there was someone who could.

8

RAELYN

"It was big, right?" Briana turned to Lacy and continued, "I mean it had to be, that smile hasn't left her for almost two days now." Sipping on her wine, she turned her suspicious gaze back to me.

"Maybe I'm just in a good mood." I shrugged my shoulders and snatched another slice of pizza from the box. After carefully removing all the olives, I took a huge bite and moaned as I savored the cheesy deliciousness.

"Are you re-enacting, Rae?" Lacy asked.

"Yeah, is that how you stuffed your mouth a few nights ago?" Brie added.

I almost choked.

Covering my lips with my hands I focused very hard on swallowing what was left in my mouth. "What the hell?" I managed to get out after a small coughing fit. By this time both of my friends were laughing so hard, tears were streaming down their faces. Every few seconds Lacy would make a lewd gesture with her hand and tongue that had Brie just howling louder.

"You two are the worst." Pushing to my feet, I glared at them both as I made my way to the kitchen to refill our drinks. After a quick glance over my shoulder to ensure I was alone, I pulled my phone from my shorts. No new messages.

I couldn't hide my disappointment. It'd been two days; if he was going to call he'd have done it by now. Shoving the phone back into my pocket, I got another spritzer for Lacy and grabbed Brie's wine bottle from the counter before heading back to the living room.

"So, are you ready to divulge all the juicy details?" Lacy asked when I sat back down.

"Who said there were juicy details?" The urge to smile again was so strong I had to take a gulp of orange juice to hide it.

"And why aren't you drinking?" Brie demanded.

I furrowed my brows and pointed at the juice bottle in my hand. "Uh…"

"She's probably trying to stay sober in case Mr. Irish phones for a booty call." Lacy downed half of her drink while pinning me with a stare that said, *'tell me I'm wrong.'*

She was half-right, though. If the other night was anything to go by, alcohol diminished my sound reasoning. I wouldn't want to do something stupid like rock up at Griffin's door and demand to know if the sex was so damn fantastic why hasn't he called.

Ugh, there was something very wrong with me.

"Well, she's not denying it." Brie deadpanned.

"The two of you—" I moved my index finger from one to the other, "—need men in your beds so you can keep your noses out of mine."

Brie took another sip of her wine before sighing dramatically. "You're not wrong. It's been ages since my pipes had a decent cleaning."

"What pipes need cleaning?" Thatcher's groggy voice drew our attention to the hallway. His mouth stretched into a yawn while he scratched the scruff under his chin. I had to bite back my laugh when Lacy and Brie openly gawked at my brother as he pushed off the wall and stalked toward us.

In typical Thatcher-fashion, his shirt was nowhere to be found and his sweatpants were riding low on his narrow hips.

If you asked me, the idiot had heard Brie was here, and he was just showing off. Thatch'd had a thing for her since high school but for some reason, he'd never made a move. Even though I'd told him I didn't mind him dating one of my friends.

"Brie is having some… *clogging issues*," I stated, feeling mighty pleased with myself.

Completely oblivious to the actual meaning behind my statement, Thatch snatched a slice of pizza and aimed his question at Brie, "You need me to come take a look?"

"I… uhm…" For the first time ever, I heard Brie stammer over her words. *Interesting.*

"Yeah, she could definitely use a hand… or two…" Lacy added. Brie all but growled as her cheeks went from rosy to beet-red. Oh, this was just too good. Both my friends had been drooling over Thatcher since he'd hit puberty. But this—whatever it was that Brie was doing—was so much more.

"I'll be happy to help," I heard my brother say. "Just let me know what day works for you." Thatch tapped the top of the couch Brie was sitting on twice before disappearing into the kitchen.

"I hate to see him go but oh, do I love to watch him leave." I barely resisted the urge to roll my eyes at Lacy's overused sentence.

A weird strangled snort sounded from the back of Brie's throat before she polished off the rest of her wine. Without sparing us a look she reached for the bottle and refilled her glass to the brim.

"Well now," Leaning back against the couch, I kept my focus on Brie. "This is… interesting."

Her narrowed gaze snapped to mine. "What?"

"You like my brother."

She held my gaze for a beat before she said, "Of course I do, he's *Thatcher Brooks*, everyone *likes* him." Her words had an edge of bitterness that piqued my curiosity.

"And all the girls want to climb him like a tree," Lacy quickly added.

Something that looked a lot like hurt flashed in Brie's eyes before she tilted her head slightly. "That too." Her wine disappeared a hell of a lot faster this time. "This has been fun, girls, but I have an early morning."

Brie was a music teacher at WF High. She'd been a bit of a piano playing sensation since the age of eight. Had even been accepted at *Julliard* but then her mom got sick and she'd decided to stay and help her dad. Putting her dreams on hold… indefinitely.

"Yeah, I better get going too." After grabbing her purse from beside the couch Lacy pushed to her feet and gave me a wink. "Besides we wouldn't want to be here when Mr. Irish *comes*."

"We wouldn't?" Brie had miraculously recovered from whatever had ailed her a few minutes ago and I was back to being their target.

I pivoted and headed for the door. "Yeah, it's definitely time for you guys to go," I shot over my shoulder. Their clicking heels and giggles following me like a shadow.

Once they reached me, both of my friends pulled me in for a hug. "You know we love you, right?"

Wrapping my arms around them, I smiled into the space between their shoulders. "I do."

After we said our goodbyes, I began tidying up the living room. It annoyed me that even while doing these mundane things my mind kept drifting to Griffin.

What was he doing?

More importantly, who was he doing it with?

At that thought, an old memory popped into my head, demanding to be in the light. Thatch and I had been in the middle of a heated argument shortly after I'd met Rob, he'd accused me of being blind and falling too hard too fast.

Maybe he was on to something?

"The girls left?"

The pizza box and napkins that I had in my hands went flying at the suddenness of my brother's voice.

Clutching at my chest, I glared at him. "What the hell, you big buffoon! My damn heart."

"What?"

My hands moved to my hips. "Don't what me and don't pretend that you don't know they're gone."

He didn't even bother denying it, simply pulled his shoulders into a shrug.

"What did you do to Brie, anyway?" I asked while I picked the trash up again.

"Me?" I could've sworn Thatch's voice went up an octave. "Did she say something."

I paused mid-bend and side-eyed my brother who was looking just a little twitchy. Now I knew something was up with the two of them. Slowly straightening, my gaze never left him. "Thatch?"

His Adam's apple bobbed up and down before his strained sentence reached my ears, "Nothing happened, okay?" The words had barely left his lips before he turned and stomped off.

I found him in the kitchen a few minutes later, staring into a mug of coffee as if it held the answer to the world's troubles. Sliding onto the stool next to him, I put my hand on his arm. "If you like her this much, why don't you just tell her?"

The big idiot looked at me as if the words coming out of my mouth were some foreign dialect. "Stay out of it, Rae," he finally gritted out.

"I'm just trying to help."

Thatch took a good swallow of coffee before he turned to face me. Leaning forward, he made sure we were at eye level. "Your meddling is neither asked for nor wanted."

Wordlessly and without blinking, I stared at him until I couldn't hold it anymore. Laughter spilled from my lips and didn't stop coming until my ribs ached. "Is that supposed to scare me? Haven't you learned that I'm not intimidated by you, you big dummy."

Jumping out of his seat, Thatcher grumbled something under his breath as he stalked off to lick his wounds. I was about to hurry after him when my phone vibrated from my back pocket. Unlocking it, I fully expected to find a teasing message from Brie or Lacy.

It wasn't.

Unknown Number: *Hi*

I stared at the phone for a second, just as I moved to press *delete* another text popped up.

Unknown Number: *I should probably have said it's Griffin *smiley face emoji**

9

GRIFFIN

I stared at me phone, willing those three dots to start jumping. When they finally did, a breath I had no idea I was holding, left me lungs in one big whoosh. It was pathetic really.

You'd think I'd never texted a woman before.

Rae: Took you long enough.

Resting me elbows on the kitchen counter, I leaned forward and started typing me reply.

Griffin: I know. Funny story, though. When I left for work, I forgot me phone at home.

Not long after I hit send did the dots start doing their thing again. When her reply was nothing more than a thinking emoji, I knew she thought I was bullshitting her. Deciding that nothing less than the truth would do, me thumbs started moving across the screen.

Griffin: You've been on me mind every minute for almost two days. I work 24-hour shifts and didn't have access to me phone, that's why I couldn't tell you that.

It took a while, but the dots finally started moving again.

Rae: It's late. Why are you texting now?

I realized then that it was almost midnight and to her, it must seem like I wanted something. Well, I did. Just not what I presumed she suspected. I typed and deleted, typed and deleted until I finally settled with:

Griffin: I want to see you.

The message showed that it was read but the dots never started jumping again. I didn't like the feeling settling inside me chest. Making me way to the living room, I collapsed onto the couch and turned on the TV. Flicking through channel after channel, I couldn't find anything to hold me attention long enough to keep me from checking me phone like a bloody idiot.

Eventually, I just switched the damn television off and headed back to bed.

Hoping like hell I'd get a small reprieve from Rae constantly running through me mind.

Standing beside the bed, I reached over me head, gripped me shirt in me hand and pulled it off. I then curled me fingers around the waistband of me sweats but before I could yank the material down, a knock sounded from the front door.

Frozen to the spot, I tilted me head and concentrated. It could be that I was imagining things because who in their right mind would show up on someone's doorstep after midnight? The only people I could think of didn't even know where I lived.

When I finally convinced myself it was nothing more than the wind, I heard it again. Louder this time. Breathing out a frustrated sigh, I stomped down the hallway to open the door. I was not even remotely prepared for what I found on the other side of it.

"Care for a midnight snack?" Smiling sweetly, Rae dangled a tub of ice cream and a bottle in front of me. Me fingers dug into the wood to the point of pain. No, I didn't want a snack; I wanted the whole damn buffet. Wearing a pair of denim cut-offs and a top that showed her shoulder and toned middle, this woman had me thoughts going in a million different directions all in the blink of an eye.

But as gorgeous as her body was, it was her smile that stole the damn show again.

"Are you just going to stand there and gawk or are you inviting me in?"

Grinning, I opened the door wider and stepped aside. "Please, come in."

Rae slowly made her way inside, stopping right in front of me. Her gaze dropped to me naked chest before steadily lifting to meet mine again. Nothing but heat shining in those pretty eyes of hers and damn, if I didn't feel it too.

She nibbled on her lip and moved closer. I tasted that kiss before our mouths even touched. Or I would have if she didn't pull back and saunter off in the direction of the kitchen.

With a sharp shake of me head, I closed the door and trailed behind her. Once we reached the kitchen, I propped me shoulder against the frame and crossed me feet at the ankles. Rae was opening cupboards and drawers until she found two tumblers and spoons. Carefully setting them on the island, she unscrewed the cap of the bottle and removed the lid off the tub of ice cream. More than a little intrigued, I stalked to where she was standing.

"This is your idea of a snack?" I eyed the rocky road ice cream and bottle of raspberry vodka.

"What's wrong with it?" Rae reached for the ice cream, but I wrapped me fingers around her wrist.

"It's an unusual combination."

"Well, I'm an unusual girl."

Her warm smile and playful wink did something to me insides. I had to clear me throat before I spoke again.

"So how do you consume this? A spoonful of ice cream followed by a shot of vodka?" I was still holding onto her wrist; she didn't seem to mind though.

"No." She shook her head, her eyes twinkling with mischief. Using her free hand, she held up her index and middle finger. "Two words… Vodka float."

"Vodka float?" I repeated slowly.

Rae let out a cute little giggle before she explained, "Yeah, it's like a soda float but with vodka and chunky ice cream. It's weird but really delicious. I learned it—"

Her words came in one ear and floated out the other. All I could focus on was her moving lips. I wanted to taste them. Feel them on me. But more importantly I wanted to be the reason they lifted into a smile. "Griffin?"

The moment our eyes connected an intense feeling curled its fists around me throat. Inside me chest, me heart thumped wildly. I was both afraid and desperate to know if she felt it too. "Why are you here?"

Her brows pulled together while she tried to pull her arm from me grip. I didn't let go. "I can leave."

Shite.

Me eyes flicked to the ceiling as I tried to string some words together that actually made sense. "Stay." I breathed out when me gaze met hers again. "I don't want you to go, Rae. I'm just curious."

Those gorgeous eyes of hers darted left and right, searching for answers to unvoiced questions. It occurred to me that there was a possibility I was reading way too much into me own feelings.

Maybe she was just looking for a repeat performance. For reasons I didn't care to explore that thought didn't sit well with me.

But if she was looking for an encore, I'd bloody well give her one she'd never forget. Me fingers around her wrist tightened, and I tugged her forward. I was inches away from those tasty looking lips when her words blew over me skin in a whisper.

"I'm not entirely sure why I came here tonight."

I pulled back slightly only to see a veil of confusion mar her features. "What are you thinking?"

She rolled her lip over her teeth, not kissing her became almost impossible. "I don't know." Her voice was soft and filled with uncertainty. "Nothing makes sense."

"I know." And I really did. When it came to Rae sense and sensibility went out the window. I shouldn't have been feeling anything but lust for a woman I barely knew. But, like a bolt of lightning, she came out of nowhere and struck me down, robbing me of me sanity.

Her tone was soft and measured when she spoke, "I guess I wanted to see if I was imagining this connection I feel to you."

I cradled her face between me palms, me voice hoarse as I asked, "And? Are you?"

"Are you going to think I'm nuts if I say I'm not?"

Instead of telling her what I thought, I showed her. Me mouth crashed to hers. The instant our lips touched; a deep groan echoed from the back of me throat. This was what I'd been craving for days.

Her kiss.

Her touch.

Everything.

I sucked on her bottom lip like a starved man before licking the inside. A sinful sound somewhere between a gasp and a moan parted her lips, and I took the opportunity to deepen the kiss.

Slick and sweet, tongue finding tongue. Tasting. Savoring. Devouring. And Rae matched me stroke for needy stroke. Driving me insane. Giving as good as she was getting. And, shite, it wasn't enough.

Hell, she could give me all she had to give and still wouldn't be enough.

I shoved me hand into her hair, tightening me fist around the silky strands. The other smoothed over the curve of her arse, tugging her flush against me.

Our kiss deepened even more.

Her hands skimmed around me waist, fingers digging into me skin. The heat of her palms incinerating the blood in me veins. I wanted more. So. Much. More.

Lifting her off the ground, I had every intention of taking her to bed, but I only got as far as the couch in the living room. With her straddling me thighs, I cupped the back of her head with me hand while the fingers of the other brushed over the bumps of her spine.

Rae's mouth moved over mine, her hands pushing into me hair and her hips rolling over me *just right*. A sound I hardly recognized vibrated through me chest and I had to inhale deeply through me nose simply because I couldn't stand to tear me mouth away from hers to catch me breath.

Me hands went to her ass to help her move over me. Harder. Faster. But she pushed off me chest and started sliding off me lap. I quickly caught her by the wrist.

"Where are you going?"

Her lips lifted into a saucy smile as she pressed her index finger against me mouth. Me tongue darted out, slicking over the tip. Rae's breath caught and the sound she made was so unbelievably erotic, I twitched with need.

"Shhh," she purred and then pushed off me lap to stand a few feet in front of me. Eyes glittering, teeth digging into her lip, she toed off her sparkly sandals.

Leaning back, I tucked me laced fingers behind me head and grinned like a bloody fool.

Rae rocked side to side, hands going to the hem of her shirt before she slowly pulled the material up. The more skin she revealed the more me fingers itched to touch. Me tongue tingled to taste.

Her shirt wasn't even all the way off and me self-control was already slipping. Me fingers flexed behind me head. The need to get up and tear her clothes off so desperate, so strong, it took every ounce of willpower I had to keep me arse parked on that couch.

But sit I did.

Even when she tossed the shirt aside and slowly turned her back to me. I remained sitting when she tortured me by gently slipping her bra strap over her shoulder. I still didn't get up when she wiggled out of her shorts and threw them at me.

It was only when she was facing me again with her fingers tucked in the waistband of her panties that I made a move. "No," I told her as I sat up. "Let me."

Her tongue darted out, making her lips wet and shiny. Padding closer, she came to a standstill between me spread legs. I reached up, fingers tracing her collarbone before brushing over the soft skin between her breasts, slowly making me way down to circle her belly button.

Her breath hitched. So did mine. Goosebumps peppered her skin while a shiver rolled down me spine. Spreading me fingers wide, I smoothed them around her waist and up her back. Digging me fingers in, I tugged her closer.

I inhaled deeply, pressing a kiss in the center of her chest. "You're so beautiful," I breathed against her skin. Me fingers curled around the waistband of her panties just as I dropped to me knees in front of her. Exactly where I needed to be considering I'd happily spend the rest of me days worshiping every inch of her body. The moment the lacy barrier disappeared me mouth was on her.

Rae's fingers speared through me hair, the tips digging into the back of me head, desperate to keep me where I was. Not that I was going anywhere until she was thoroughly satisfied.

Me fingers dug into her skin as I doubled me efforts. Her thighs shook and a second later me name rolled off her tongue. Holding on to her, I gently guided us back to the couch. Me movements were jerky and hurried as I shoved me sweats down me legs.

That first second when I finally, *finally*, got to lose myself in the warmth of her body again, I couldn't move.

This moment, this thing between us, felt big. Impossibly big. Like the pieces that made up me life was shifting and realigning only to never be the same again. And I had absolutely no hope of understanding any of it.

"Griff—" Rae started but I cut her off when I pushed me hips up. Hard. "Mhmm."

We moved together like we'd been doing this dance for years. Like her body was made for me and mine for her.

When I felt her climb close to the edge, I brushed me fingertips over her cheek and whispered, "Look at me, Rae." Her lids parted slowly, revealing those incredible deep blue irises that snatched the air right out of me lungs.

When her world finally exploded, I was right there with her. Hooking me hand around her neck, I pulled her face to mine. Fusing our mouths together in a kiss that I felt all the way to the bottom of me soul.

This should be scary.

Should freak me the hell out.

Instead, a strange feeling of calm washed over me. I couldn't explain it. Didn't want to. But when Rae slumped against me, and me arms wrapped around her, I just knew that this woman was at the center of it all.

10

RAELYN

I was losing my mind.

Or could it be my heart? With my face buried in the crook of Griffin's neck, I mentally conceded that it might be a little of both. I was very aware of the fact that I barely knew him, but somehow being with him felt… different.

Maybe even right?

It was also possible that my post-orgasm brain was the one doing the thinking. Closing my eyes, I snuggled deeper into him when the sound of my rumbling tummy ruined the moment. I felt myself blush all the way to my toes. Squeezing my lids tighter, I begged the ground to open up and swallow me in.

No such luck.

Griffin pushed a hand into my hair, urging me to lift my head and look at him. When I did, the grin on his lips had my heart doing cartwheels. "We never did have that snack, did we?"

I lifted my shoulder into a shrug. "Well, you did."

Those eyes of his turned even darker as his gaze dropped to my chest before returning to mine. "Aye, I did. Somehow, I'm ravenous again."

The intensity in his irises stole my breath. Not once in all my life had a man looked at me the way Griffin was looking at me. The way it made me feel, scared me. I could hear my heart thundering away as his mouth came closer and closer.

As much as I wanted that kiss, I didn't dare take it. I needed to sort through whatever it was that was going on inside of me. Because it definitely wasn't normal to feel this way about someone after only knowing them for a few days.

Ducking what I knew would've been a delicious kiss, I slipped off his lap and started gathering my clothes. Brows pulled into a deep frown; his gaze remained on me as I haphazardly pulled on item after item.

It took a while, but he finally pushed to his feet too. Still staring at me with that confused look in his eyes, his mouth opened but instead of saying what he wanted to say, he snapped his lips shut and pulled on his sweats.

"Are you ready to have your taste buds assaulted in the best way?" I hoped my attempt at making light of the situation worked. But knew it hadn't when Griffin stalked toward me; movements sure and steady, his face serious.

I held my breath.

He was standing so close; I could simply reach out and touch him. I wanted that so badly I had to curl my hands into tight fists. Long agonizing seconds ticked by as he just stood there, his dark gaze boring into mine.

My heart stuttered while the butterflies in my stomach fluttered wildly.

Griffin moved fast; taking my face between his palms and lowering his head so he could look straight into my eyes. Into my soul. "You feel it too, don't you?"

I had to swallow twice before I could squeak out, "What?"

He shook his dark head. "No games. It's just you and me here, and I know you feel the pull between us. I saw it in your eyes right before I saw uncertainty seep in."

"This is crazy."

"Maybe."

I tried to pull away from him, but he wasn't having it. "What we're feeling is lust."

"Say it again, acushla." His face inched even closer. "With more conviction this time. Maybe you'll believe yourself." The pad of his thumb swept over my skin in a ghost of a touch. "And it was only lust that made you come here in the middle of the night? All that talk earlier about feeling connected was total bullshit then?"

This man saw right through any wall I tried to erect.

"Griffin," I pleaded. "It can't be anything more than that, we hardly know each other."

His eyes searched mine for a few seconds before he said, "Let's rectify that. You can ask me anything and I swear to answer it honestly."

Was this guy for real? I was used to men who'd rather endure a root canal than sit and talk. That old proverb popped into my head: *When something seems too good to be true, it probably is*. Right now, Griffin seemed to be just that.

Warning bells should've rung.

Either I was hearing impaired or there really weren't any. Could it be? Was it even possible to fall for someone within seconds of meeting them?

"You're overthinking." Griffin's voice drew my attention back to him. He wasn't wrong. I just didn't want to fall for another Rob. "I tell you what," he went on. "Let's get you something to eat before we continue this conversation."

My gaze roamed over his face, a million things fighting to be heard and said at once. But somehow the only one that came tumbling out of my mouth was, "Okay."

His hands smoothed down my arms until he could lace our fingers. Silently we made our way to the kitchen only to find that the ice cream had melted. "Guess you won't be trying a vodka float after all."

Griffin's lips lifted into a playful smile that didn't quite make it to his eyes. "You'll just have to introduce me to your strange midnight snack some other time," he said. His voice was so serious, I could only stare at him as he binned the melted dairy and started scavenging the cupboards.

"This will have to do," he said, producing a bag of Doritos and a packet of gummy sweets. After grabbing two bottles of water from the fridge, he slid onto the stool opposite me.

I took the offered water, downed half of it and put a decent dent in the packet of chips before I blurted out, "My brother seems to think I have a bad habit of falling too fast."

When my word-vomit was met with a raised eyebrow, I took a breath. "A little over a year ago I'd met someone and despite everyone's warnings, I started a relationship with him. It got serious really fast—for me at least."

My gaze dropped to my folded hands resting on the countertop. I started fidgeting with my fingers as memories of my stupidity assaulted me. Before they

sucked me in though, the warmth of Griffin's palm
against my arm registered.

When I looked up, the expression in his was so gentle
it almost made my heart ache. "I don't have to know
the rest."

I stopped fidgeting and placed my hand on his. "While
I'd been dreaming of a big wedding, Rob had been
scheming up a way to take what little savings I'd had."
My eyes skittered to the door before they connected
with Griffin's again. "That wasn't the worst of it,
though."

A few curses fell from his lips in his mother tongue
which I found oddly endearing.

"My friends and I wanted to try out a new burger place
one night. We'd just grabbed our drinks when I'd
spotted Rob sitting in one of the booths lining the back
wall." I could still feel a small sting of betrayal at the
memory.

"Of course I walked over to say hi… Only he wasn't
alone. His wife of almost six years was sitting with
him. His heavily pregnant wife, I might add."

"What?" He sounded completely mortified.

I let out a nervous giggle. "Yeah, turned out while his
wife lived a few towns over, he'd pretended to work
for a financial company here in West Kirksin. The
closest he came to working with money was when he'd

cleverly syphoned away some of my savings. Which I didn't know about until much later."

Griffin's eyes turned a scary shade of almost black. "What happened at the burger joint?"

The heat creeping into my cheeks couldn't be helped. It was equal amounts anger and embarrassment.

"When I… uh… walked up to the table he pretended he didn't know me. Swore to his wife I was some crazy girl trying to hook up with him."

"Cic maith se tóin atá dlíth air."

I blinked and blinked again. "What does that mean?"

He shook his head, frustration pulling his brows together. "He needs a kick up the arse." Griffin jerked his chin in my direction. "What happened then?"

"My milkshake landed in his lap while Lacy and Brie dunked theirs over his head. He was arrested for fraud not long after this happened—which was how I found out about my savings." I lifted my shoulders. "And as far as I know his wife left him and moved away."

His nostrils flared with the deep drag of air he took to his lungs. I thought he was going to say something, but he ended up emptying his bottle of water.

I chewed on the inside of my cheek, searching for the right words to adequately express myself. "You can understand why I'm having a hard time trusting my own judgment right now," I finally said.

"Aye."

He removed his hand from my arm to rake his fingers through his hair. I also noticed that he avoided making eye contact with me. Suddenly sharing my stupid story seemed like the worst idea ever. I slid off the stool and pushed the feeling of disappointment as far away as I could manage.

"I should go."

Immediately his gaze snapped to mine, confusion creasing his forehead. "You want to leave?"

No, I didn't. "It's late."

His eyebrow arched again, "So?"

"I'm sure you have to get up early for work. I know I do." I actually had the day off, he didn't need to know that, though.

He pushed to his feet, that intense look in his eyes again. "You running away, Rae?" *What the hell?* I opened my mouth to ask him just that, but he silenced me with a shake of his head. "I get it, you've been hurt."

He stalked toward me with slow determined strides until we were toe to toe. Gripping my chin between his fingers, he guided my gaze to his. "I'm not asking for your trust. All I want is an opportunity to earn it."

11

GRIFFIN

This wasn't me. I didn't jump into things without weighing the consequences first. This wasn't planned, it wasn't thought out, but dammit, if it didn't feel right. I couldn't explain it, from the moment I'd laid eyes on this woman, I'd known she was different. Logic warned me to pull back, assess what I was feeling. Only, I was done running and hiding.

If I was destined to crash and burn, I'd go willingly.

Rae's widened eyes scanned over me face before our gazes locked. Those beautiful blue irises of hers reflecting every single thing I felt in me core.

"This is crazy," she repeated. The words falling from her lips in a mere whisper.

"So you've said."

I watched her work down a few swallows before she voiced something else I felt too. "I'm scared, Griffin." When she pulled away from me touch, I reluctantly let her go. "We went from having fun to something else entirely in the blink of an eye." She paced back and forth, her teeth worrying her bottom lip.

The need to walk over and wrap me arms around her was strong. I almost gave in and did just that when a little voice in me head cautioned me to give her the space she needed to make sense of everything.

Not that much sense could be made unless you believed that love at first sight really did exist.

"I'm scared too." I kept me voice steady as I slowly approached her. "I know the difference between lust and wanting something more." When I reached her, I took her hand in mine. "This isn't lust, Rae. Not even close."

Her eyes narrowed but at least she didn't pull away from me. "Oh yeah? Didn't we just have crazy monkey sex?"

Biting me cheek, I kept me grin from spreading. "Aye, that we did. The point that you are missing, acushla, is that the *crazy monkey sex* isn't the only thing I want from you. I want *all* of you. Tell me your fears, so I can make them mine. Your hopes and dreams, I want to make those come true. I want—"

Before I could finish she started shaking her head furiously. "This is too much."

She wasn't wrong. This was too much and not enough at the same time. Again, I cradled her face between me palms. "You're right." I lowered me head until our noses almost touched. "If you can honestly tell me that you don't feel it too, I won't say another word." Rae opened her mouth to speak but I silenced her by sliding me thumb over her lips. "But, if it's there and we both feel it, why not explore it?"

She was really thinking about what I'd just said, I could see it in her eyes. I just hoped when she opened her mouth to speak, she'd voice the words I needed to hear. Rae's gaze roamed over me face, I sucked in a breath and held it.

"Okay." Everything else she'd said tonight had had a hint of uncertainty to it. However, this single word that slipped from her lips, didn't. There was nothing else left to say, words were just empty syllables without a deed to back them up.

So, I lowered me mouth to hers in a kiss that tasted so different than the others.

Her fear. Her hesitancy. Her want. I could taste them all. Mix that with everything I was feeling, and you had one powerful cocktail of want and need.

I kissed her deep and slow as her arms banded tightly around me waist. Me fingers pushed into her hair. The silky tresses twisted and tangled in me grip, but I couldn't bring myself to let go. I didn't want to give her one second of sanity in case she changed her mind. She was mine.

I needed her to stay mine.

I was very aware that I was behaving like an uncivilized caveman, I was also way past rationalizing me feelings when it came to Rae. If at all possible, our kiss deepened even more. I swear I felt each stroke of her tongue all the way to me soul.

The needy little moan that sounded from the back of her throat was equivalent to fuel being thrown onto an already raging fire. Without removing me mouth from hers, I lifted her and walked us to the bedroom.

This time there was no slow seduction. If I could have ripped every stitch of fabric covering her body, I would've. When there was nothing between us, I descended on her like a beast ready to devour his prey. Which I was.

With every roll of me hips, I made her mine all over again. When her voice was hoarse and our lungs out of breath, I collapsed beside her. Gathering her in me arms, she rested her head against me chest.

I stared at the ceiling amazed at how the odd turns life sometimes took always managed to lead us to the place we were supposed to be. With Rae safely tucked in beside me, I gave into the heaviness of me lids. I just hoped when morning came, I wouldn't wake to find that this was nothing more than a dream.

***

"You didn't run away."

Her smile was even brighter than the sun filtering in through the curtains. "You sound surprised."

"Pleasantly so. Especially since I woke up to a cold bed last time." I reached forward and wrapped a strand of her hair around me finger. "What time do you have to be at work?"

"About that." The slightest blush stole her cheeks. "I'm not going in today." When the only response I gave her was a raised eyebrow, she added, "I thought what I'd told you was too much, so my brain conjured up the best way to make a quick exit."

With a chuckle I shook me head. "I'm going to have to keep me eye on you." Not being able to resist, I dropped a quick kiss to her lips before I slipped from the bed. I felt her eyes on me when I reached into the cupboard to grab a t-shirt.

"Come on," I said as I tossed her the shirt. "We need to put back all the calories you burned." Rae picked up the material but made no move to put it on.

"Something wrong?"

She ran her fingers over the badge printed on the cotton before casting a confused gaze me way. "You're the new lieutenant at Sixty-Three." It wasn't a question, rather a statement. One she didn't seem very happy about too.

"What? Do you have something against firefighters?"

Rae shook her head before tucking a strand of hair behind her ear. "I don't, but I think things just got a little more complicated."

"Complicated?"

Her gaze stayed on me as the words fell from her lips, "Thatcher Brooks is my brother."

It would have been more believable if she'd told me that the sun had fallen from the sky. There was no way me sinfully sweet Rae was related to that *feishí*.

I walked back to the bed. "So, your brother and I don't see eye to eye. It will make for some awkward moments, it doesn't make me less interested in you." It occurred to me then that this could be a deal breaker for her. After all, family should always be most important.

"He really doesn't like you. If he knew you were the guy I'm seeing, he'd lose it." Rae reached for me hand and pulled me down next to her. "Good thing I know how to handle Thatch." The smile on her lips did funny things to me heart. "All I ask, let me be the one to tell him."

I looked down at our connected hands before I lifted her fingers to press a kiss to them. "I'm not the kiss-and-tell type." Before all rational thoughts drowned in her beauty, I pushed to me feet. "Now come on." I tugged on her arm. "You need food."

"Aaah and here I was thinking a girl could survive on sex and kisses alone." Rae playfully batted her lashes at me.

"Woman, if that were the case, I'd have you chained to the bed."

She rolled her eyes in a very dramatic fashion and mumbled, "Promises, promises."

I pounced so fast; she didn't even see me coming. Gripping her wrists in me hands, I held them above her head. "I didn't quite catch what you said." She tried to wiggle her hips, but I had her in a vice grip.

"I said—" Just as she began to speak, I lowered me head and rubbed me whiskers against her neck. I knew from all our *crazy monkey sex*—as Rae had so eloquently put it—it was a tender spot for her. "Wait, no!" she squealed.

Her attempt to break free only spurred me on. It didn't take long until her laughter echoed through the room. It also didn't take long for me to realize how much I loved the sound of it.

"Stop," she begged right before another bout of laughter overtook her. "Please!"

Taking pity on her, I lifted me head. The carefree look on her face hit me right in the center of me chest. Okay, maybe a little to the left. "You ready to have breakfast now?"

"Yes!"

With a chuckle, I pushed off the bed and waited for her to slip me shirt over her head. She almost drowned in it, but somehow still managed to look sexy as hell. We were in the kitchen a few moments later, working side by side like it was the most natural thing in the world. Rae prepared the toast while I scrambled some eggs and mashed a few avocados.

"Tell me about your family?" she asked quietly.

When the avocado reached the perfect consistency— smooth and creamy—I placed the bowl on the counter next to the toaster. I couldn't resist pressing me lips to her forehead before I walked back to the stove to check on the eggs. I pulled the pan off the heat and turned to face her. Crossing me arms in front of me, I started, "Well we're an odd bunch. Me da used to be a firefighter and me ma is a sheep farmer."

Rae's eyes went big with amazement. "A sheep farmer?"

"Aye, she inherited the farm from her *daideó.* I've never seen a woman work as hard as she does." Warmth seeped into me heart just thinking about me family. The decision to move away from them was one of the hardest I'd made, not that it'd been mine to make.

"Any siblings?" There was a small smile playing on her lips while she plied the toast with creamy avocado.

"One brother, Collin. He is a painter, doing really well for himself too. There weren't many opportunities for him to grow his talent in Ireland. He's younger and easily distracted so me da didn't want him coming to the States alone."

Rae stopped mid-spread and stared at me. I wasn't sure I deserved the wonder shining in her eyes. "You gave up your life in Ireland so your brother could go after his dream?"

"I can be a firefighter anywhere."

"You're amazing." Heat crept into me cheeks; I didn't like the feeling one bit. For a few seconds, we just stared at each other, everything else melting away. It was me and her in this little bubble of what I presumed heaven looked like. Nothing and no one else mattered. The spell was finally broken when she cleared her throat, "So, uhm, your brother he's still—" her brows drew together. "You never did tell me where you moved from."

I pushed off the counter and pulled two plates from the cupboard. Just thinking about Sault Point had me thoughts going to Adam and his family. I didn't want her to see the shame in me eyes. "City life wasn't for me, I moved to a little town about three hours north from here not long after Collin graduated and got himself settled."

If Rae noticed the shift in me demeanor she didn't mention it. "Oh, I couldn't do city life either." She continued to load the bread with the avocado. "West Kirksin born and raised."

"You've lived here your entire life?"

"Yup."

"That explains it, then." I glanced over me shoulder in time to see her brows knit together.

"Explains what?"

"The night we met; you knew I was a newcomer. I thought maybe you were some sort of heavy drinker who lived in the bar."

"What?"

I tried to hide me smile but failed miserably. Unfortunately, before I could tell Rae I was just joking with her, a slice of avocado toast hit me in the chest. That laugh that had already worked its way to me heart filled the room again. I aimed me raised eyebrow at Rae. Shaking with laughter, she held up both hands.

"I'm sorry… I didn't think it would really hit you…"

"Oh, you're gonna pay for that."

"I said I was—" I started stalking toward her, she held her hands in front of her as she walked backward.

"Wait! You stop right there."

When she was backed up against the fridge, I rushed forward. Placing one hand next to her head, I dragged a finger of the other through the smeared avocado on me chest. I looked her straight in the eyes, those deep blue depths pulling me in so fast I almost forgot what I wanted to do.

Almost.

A finger armed with green creaminess swiped over her little button nose before moving to her forehead and cheeks. Rae pressed her palms against me chest, trying to push me away. I dug me heels in and continued to paint her face green.

"There." Stepping back, I admired me handywork.

"Pretty as a picture."

She pulled her nose up and planted her hands on her hips. "Are you satisfied now?"

I chuckled and shook me head. "Not even close, but it will have to do for now."

12

RAELYN

As I pulled into the driveway, I was certain the smile on my lips wasn't going anywhere anytime soon. I turned the key, shutting off the engine, but instead of getting out, I just sat there processing the last fifteen hours of my life.

Had it really been just a few hours?

I dropped my head to the steering wheel and laughed. It wasn't one of those oh-shit-what-have-I-done laughs either, it was one of pure happiness. The moment I stopped questioning it and embraced how right things with Griffin felt, was absolutely liberating.

The possibility that he was just another Rob was there in the back of my mind. The thing was if I kept erring on the side of caution, was I really living? The answer was no. Not just no, but hell no.

I've never felt more alive than I had during the hours spent with Griffin.

My smiles weren't forced, my laughter wasn't laced with sadness. Most importantly, I just was. No masks, no pretending. I liked it. I liked him… A lot more than I should have at this stage but who cared, right?

I got out of the car and made my way into the house. Knowing Thatcher, he was probably pacing the living room waiting for my return, so he could scold me. I used to like living with my brother.

Until now.

After I sucked in a fortifying breath, I pushed through the front door. As suspected, the first thing I saw was my idiot brother standing with his feet spread and those thick arms of his folded across his chest.

When he opened his mouth, I silenced him with a sharp shake of my head. "Not now, Thatch."

The veins in his neck bulged as redness started to seep into his cheeks, "Not now? That's all you have to say? I have been sick with worry." He threw his arms in the air. "Hell, I probably called every person in this town looking for you."

"Dramatic much?" I tossed my keys into the apple shaped bowl next to the door and attempted to get further into the house. When I tried to push past Thatch, he curled his fingers around my upper arm to stop me. "Thatcher," I warned.

"Where have you been, Rae?"

I twisted until he had no choice but to let me go. His intentions were good, his heart in the right place, but I was sick of it. Squaring my shoulders, I tilted my chin, so I could look him straight in the eye when I said, "I went to see a guy about an itch I needed scratched."

My brother's brows furrowed, "You're seeing someone? Who is it?"

"You don't know him." Okay, yeah, this would've been the perfect time to tell my dear brother that the guy I was sleeping with was also the same guy who got the job he'd wanted. I didn't have the guts or energy to do it, though.

Thatcher was already pissed off which meant he wouldn't see reason.

"I know everyone in this town." With his eyes narrowed he tried to stare me down.

"You don't know *him*," I repeated. Pivoting, I marched toward my bedroom hoping we were done with the conversation. Lady luck wasn't on my side unfortunately, Thatcher was right on my heels.

"Fine, I don't know him." He propped his shoulder against the doorframe, his gaze burning holes in me while I hooked my phone up to the charger. "But do you?" The question stung. This time it was my turn to narrow my eyes at him. Not phased, he went on, "Remember what happened the last time you fell for someone you hardly knew."

I jumped up from where I was sitting on the edge of the bed and stomped toward him. "How could I ever forget?" I asked, arms spread, palms up. "When you do such a bang-up job at reminding me every chance you get."

"You think it was fun for me to come home to find you curled up on your bed, sobbing your eyes out?"

"You're being—"

"If caring about you is being dramatic, I wear the label with pride." Thatcher pushed off the frame and came to stand in front of me. He cupped my shoulders as he spoke, "You're all I have left, Raelyn. I won't apologize for worrying about you." Without warning, he yanked me forward and almost crushed me in his embrace. "I should've been there to protect you."

I hugged my brother back. "It's not your job to protect me, Thatch. I'm a big girl and I need to make mistakes. It's the only way we learn."

Bringing his hands up to cup my shoulders again, he pushed me back slightly. "I hate it when you're smarter than me."

"Really? I thought you'd be used to it by now."

Thatcher shook his head as he walked backward. "I hope this poor shmuck knows you're a cheeky little firecracker."

"Oh, he does."

"Good." My brother's face turned serious. "He better treat you right, Rae."

I swallowed down the sudden lump in my throat. "I have a feeling about him, Thatch. But if I'm wrong, you have my permission to teach him a lesson."

"That's more like it." He flashed his teeth in a wide smile before tapping the frame twice. "Good night."

***

With my hand on the door, I paused at the entrance of our favorite coffee shop. I was meeting up with Brie for our weekly one-on-one coffee date. As much as the three of us loved spending time together, I found that Brie opened up more when it was just the two of us. At first, I invited her for coffee every other week, it didn't take long to turn into a weekly thing, though. After reminding myself a few times that whatever was happening with Thatch and my friend was none of my business, I pushed through the door and scanned the tables. I wasn't surprised when I spotted Brie sipping on a steaming mug of tea with her nose buried in a book.

I quickly ordered a coffee and two chocolate chip muffins before joining her at the table. "Are you at the good parts yet?" Without lifting her head, she flicked her gaze my way. It irritated her to no end that Lacy and I were only interested in hearing about the saucy bits.

One perfectly shaped eyebrow arched. "Really?"

With feigned innocence, I lifted my shoulders, "What?"

Brie closed her book and carefully moved it to the side. "One of these days I am going to force you to sit down and read so you can see romance novels are so much more than porn for women."

I really shouldn't tease her, but I just couldn't help myself. Plus, I kind of owed her for the razing she and Lacey gave me the other night. "Is that so? And how many tips have you utilized from these novels, mmm?" Her answer came in the form of two bright red spots on her cheeks. With a giggle, I reached across the table and squeezed her hand. "I'm just teasing you."

Relaxing into my seat, I added, "Besides, I might need some of those tips myself."

There was a huge smile on her face when she said, "You're horrible." After the waiter served my coffee and the two muffins, Brie leaned forward and asked, "So, where were you? Thatch called yesterday sounding more grumpy than usual."

As I tore a piece of cakey goodness off, a very unladylike snort escaped me. "He wasn't grumpy, he was pissed off because I didn't give him an itinerary of my daily activities."

"Rae, you know why he's like that."

I let out a sigh. "Yeah, it's just so frustrating. A girl can't go out at midnight, get laid, and snag herself a boyfriend in the process without getting the third degree."

"Hold up." Brie's eyes widened. "You used the B-word."

Chewing on my lip, I nodded. "At least I think that's where we're at."

"You think?" My friend's concern was written all over her features. She reached forward and placed her hand on mine. "Rae—"

"I know what you're going to say," I interrupted. "I realize this is moving at the speed of light and I am very aware of the fact that my track record is horrible. But I am going to tell you the same thing I told Thatch; I have a feeling about this guy."

Briana regarded me for a few seconds before she nodded slowly. "If he turns out to be a dickhead, I am relieving him of his."

"You might have to fight my idiot-brother on that." I pulled a face as I recalled another reason why my brother would only be too happy to rain down punches on Griffin. "There's something else."

"Uh oh."

"You know how I told you that Thatch got passed up for a promotion?"

Brie's eyes went wide, and she covered her mouth with her hands. "Oh no."

"Oh yes," I fired back. "Griffin is the new LT at Sixty-Three."

"Does Thatcher know?"

I turned my head to the window in time to spot a young mother pushing a stroller while having an animated conversation with the toddler walking next to her. "He just knows I'm seeing someone," I said when I faced Brie again.

"Rae, you know even though I joke a lot I would never purposefully stick my nose in your business—" she took a deep breath before she rushed on, "—but you have to tell Thatch. Sooner would be better than later." She was absolutely right, I just needed to find the damn courage to do it before my brother found out on his own.

13

GRIFFIN

Like an idiot, I grinned at the little rectangle screen in me hand. When me phone had beeped a few seconds ago, I was hoping it'd be a text from Rae. What I got when I opened the message was so much better. Rae's beautiful face filled me screen, her lips all puckered up ready for a kiss.

Me phoned buzzed again.

Rae: *Can it be tomorrow night already?*

I was smiling so hard, me cheeks ached. Glancing at the digital clock on me truck's radio, I figured I had about 10 minutes before I had to head into the station. Me thumbs started moving across the screen.

Me: *Miss me bad, huh?*

Her reply came immediately.

Rae: *Maybe *winky face emoji**

I still couldn't believe how fast things had escalated with this woman nor could I explain how everything felt as if it was meant to happen this way. The only certainty was that it had been a long time since I'd felt happiness like this.

If ever.

Me: *I miss you too, Rae.*

An engine roaring past me had me looking up from me phone. I scanned me surroundings and caught a glimpse of me reflection in the rearview mirror. Shaking me head, I muttered, "You've got it bad." The words had barely left me lips when me phone sounded again. I couldn't look at the thing fast enough which just proved me point.

Rae: *My friends would like to meet you; would that be OK?*

It was more than okay, and I told her that in me next reply. When me phone started ringing, I assumed it was Rae who wanted to tell me where and when I would be meeting her friends.

"Do I need protection?" I asked when I pressed the device against me ear.

"Griffin?" Me blood turned to ice as Mildred's voice filtered through the line.

I am not proud to admit I briefly entertained the idea of hanging up and powering down me phone. I didn't, though. "I'm here, Mildred." The strain in me voice burned me throat or maybe it was shame.

The woman at the other end of the line took in a few sharp breaths. "You just left without saying goodbye." I hung me head and pinched the bridge of me nose. "I know."

"Do you know how it felt when I knocked on your door only to find the place empty?" The hurt in her voice almost did me in. I deserved the sting I felt in me chest and in the back of me eyes.

"I'm sorry," me reply was lame, but I meant it. "I was—*am*—having a hard time. With so much loss surrounding me, I was losing myself too."

"You should have talked to us, Griffin." There was a moment of silence and then, "I am not mad that you left like you did. I'm hurt that you didn't trust us enough to share your pain. I don't care that you're not my blood, you're my son too."

Well, shite. What was I supposed to say to that? That ache in the left side of me chest got so painful that I had to rub the spot through the material of me shirt. Me nose burned and the back of me eyes stung something fierce.

"I'm an idiot because I didn't want to burden you or Heath. I know how difficult it's been for you." And that was putting it mildly. When Adam and Zoe were younger some things had come out that just about ripped the family apart. As a result, Zoe started acting out. The more her parents tried to reel her in, the more out of control she became.

Then there was the fire.

At the time, they'd lived in Texas City, but when tragedy struck, they moved to Sault Point to be with their son.

"Your troubles will never burden us." Mildred's soft words pulled me back to our conversation. "Don't apologize for putting yourself first."

I pinched me eyes and cleared me throat, "How is he?"

"Not good. He's scared the nurse away, and he doesn't want me or Heath living there with him." The pain in her voice was so raw, it felt like a hand had reached through the phone and squeezed me chest.

After the fire Adam had refused to leave the house. Soon it had escalated to him holing himself up in the bedroom. Every time the Carlisles hired someone to take care of him and the house, he'd find a way to run them off.

"He'll get better," I promised. "Maybe not now but he will."

Mildred sniffled. "I have to believe you're right." There was a short pause and when she spoke again her tone was cautious, "When are you off again?"

"I'm just about ready to start a new shift, so in twenty-four hours, I suppose."

"Do you think you'll be coming back to Sault Point anytime soon?" she asked hopefully. "Just to visit, of course."

"I'll come see you next week, okay?"

With an I love you I felt I hadn't earned, we said our
goodbyes. I tucked me phone inside me pocket and
headed for the station, intending to drown myself in
work until I felt anything else than the guilt gnawing
on me insides.

Two hours later, I was buried in the previous day's
report when a knock sounded on me open door. I
looked up to see Chief Abbott filling the doorway.
"How are you holding up?" he asked as he seated
himself in front of me desk.

I set the paper down and leaned back in me seat. "Still
observing everything, sir."

He made a humming sound, eyes scanning over the
surface of the desk before meeting mine. "Brooks
giving you trouble?"

I took a breath through me nose. "Nothing I can't
handle."

To me surprise the Chief started chuckling. When he
noticed me confused stare, he lifted a shoulder.
"Nothing happens in my station without me knowing
about it. He let you walk back from the hospital." He
dropped his elbows to his knees and leaned forward.
"I'm curious, why didn't you write him up?"

"He's just puffing his chest, sir. I took his job." *And
I'm sleeping with his sister.* I still had trouble
connecting the two of them.

"The boys of Sixty-Three are mighty fine men, but some of them can be a bit… let's say… temperamental. I get that you're still finding your footing here, but son, I'm afraid you're gonna have to show these boys why you're their lieutenant."

Chief Abbott pushed to his feet and gave me a brusque nod before he ambled out of me office. Apparently, me morning had gone from bad to worse. I pulled me phone from me pocket, if anything was going to make me feel better, it was Rae's voice.

Just as me finger descended on the green button, the ear-splitting sound of the firehouse alarm sliced through the air. With a sigh, I threw the device on the table before sprinting to the change house to get into me gear.

Lights flashing, siren blaring we made our way out of the station but not before Thatcher gave me one hell of a look. I shook me head because this pissing contest was getting old. The *feisí* needed to get over himself and realize there were more important things than his inflated ego.

"Hey," Nathan sitting next to me nudged me shoulder. "A bunch of us are going out for a couple of drinks tomorrow night. You wanna join?"

I was about to say yes when I remembered that Rae wanted me to meet her friends. I shook me head, "I have plans."

"Are you shitting me?" He looked both amused and confused. "You've been in town for what… five minutes and already you have a date?" Nathan shook his head. "How do you do it?"

I flashed him a way-too-cocky smirk. "Must be me Irish-charm."

"Send some of that my way, will ya?"

"No amount of charm in the world will get *you* laid, man." George, one of the probies mocked. A few more light-hearted insults were thrown Nathan's way and pretty soon we were snickering. It felt good to be laughing with me fellow firefighters. If I had any say in it, Sixty-Three was going to be me home for a long time. So getting along with these boys was a necessity. The rig rolled to a stop at the scene. It was another medical call—surprisingly we handled a lot more of these than actual fires.

When George, Nathan, and I headed into the apartment we found our patient slumped over on the couch, clutching her chest. Her breathing came in quick successions. I glanced over me shoulder and mouthed for Nathan to call for an ambulance before I slowly dropped to me haunches in front of the woman. Placing me hand on her knee, I drew her attention. When her panicked gaze met mine, she sputtered, "I… think… having… heart attack."

"I know it's hard, but take a deep breath for me, okay?" She nodded. "Me buddy over there—" I lifted me chin in Nathan's direction. "—has already made the call, the EMT's will be here in just a bit."

Instead of nodding, the woman gripped me wrist and squeezed. She looked even more panicked than before. "No!" She was shaking her head furiously. "No."

I patted the hand cutting off the circulation in me arm. "We want to help you."

"No ambulance. I don't want to go."

I couldn't even remember how many times this had happened before. Ambulances and elderly patients didn't mix. A little old lady had told me once she was afraid she'd never go home if she left in an ambulance. Still patting her hand, I calmly said, "It's important we get you to the hospital. What if I went in the ambulance with you?"

Her head bobbed slightly, her voice shaky. "You'd… do… that?"

"Of course I will." I flashed her a smile and pointed toward a table stacked with framed photographs. "You can tell me all about your family on the drive over." Her lips twitched like she was attempting to smile as she finally loosened her grip on me wrist. She didn't let go though. Not even when the EMTs arrived five minutes later. She still held on to me when she was rolled to the waiting ambulance.

Before we pulled away, I told Nathan to have the rig pick me up at the hospital. I just hoped Thatcher didn't pull another stunt on me.

***

Fuming, I stomped into the station. The first person I saw also happened to be the one I was having murderous thoughts about. Thatcher was busy cleaning the rig. With every step I took, rational thought and calm left me.

"What's your damn problem?" I gritted out when I reached the idiot.

Brooks straightened; his mouth stretched into a grin. I curled me fingers into a fist. It took all me restraint not to ram it through this piece of shite's skull.

"Thought you might like the fresh air."

Tick. Tick. Tick. I was one tick away from bloody exploding. I took a step forward and got right up in his face, "This little tantrum you're throwing is exactly why I am lieutenant and you're not."

"Screw you!"

Me blood was burning hot with anger and frustration. So much frustration. "I should be writing you up. Shite! If it wasn't for—" by some miracle I managed to stop before I mentioned Rae's name. Shaking me head, I took a step back. "This is your last warning, Brooks. Next time you disobey orders, it's your head."

As I turned and marched to me office, I spotted Chief Abbott. His contemplative gaze flitting between me and Thatcher.

Shite! How much worse could this bloody shift get?

14

RAELYN

"We don't have to do this," I said softly.

We were sitting in front of the bar, ready to meet up with Lacy and Brie. But Griffin seemed miles away. I'd suspected something was off when I went over to his place to get ready and he didn't even attempt to get me into bed first.

The way he was just staring at the entrance had me convinced something wasn't right. Nervous tension licked its way down my spine. I shoved it aside and scooted closer to Griffin and placed my hand on his thigh.

"Let me call them and schedule for some other time."

His big hand covered mine, tangling our fingers together. Draping his free arm over my shoulder, he gently brushed his fingertips back and forth over my bare skin. My body shuddered. "I want to meet your friends."

"You're sure? 'Cause it's okay if you don't."

The hand on my shoulder slid up and up until his fingers pushed into my hair. "They're *your* friends, of course, I want to get to know them." He pressed his lips against my forehead before resting his head against mine.

An uneasy feeling sparked at the base of my skull and worked its way through my veins. "You promised me honesty," I whispered. "I can tell something is going on."

He pulled back, those soul-searching eyes of his roaming all over my face. "I have a lot on my mind, acushla. I want to tell you it all, but this is not the time nor the place." Griffin lowered his mouth to mine in a kiss so achingly sweet it made my heart squeeze. "Tonight, we have fun, hmm?"

After one more bone-melting kiss, we finally headed inside. I adored how he immediately laced our fingers together and kept me close. After a quick scan, I spotted the girls sitting at the same table we'd occupied the night I'd met Griffin. A small smile tugged at my lips. I squeezed his hand and motioned to Lacy and Brie. "There they are."

He followed my gaze and grinned. "You go ahead while I get the drinks."

I pushed through the patrons only to be met with squealing when I reached my friends. "Oh my goodness, Rae," Lacy wrapped her fingers around my wrist and yanked me into the chair next to her. "You guys look so stinking cute together. And—" she gestured toward my outfit. "I'm loving this."

I adjusted the top of my baby-blue tube dress and smiled sheepishly. Normally I was a jeans and t-shirt kinda girl, but I wanted to look nice tonight. When I saw this dress in the store window this afternoon, I just had to have it.

"She's wearing a dress so she and Mr. Irish can sneak off and have a quickie in the bathroom." My gaze snapped to Briana who was looking way too smug for my liking.

"I can hear it now," Lacy added. "*Oh yes, Griffin, do it. Take me now with your big Irish*—"

Yeah, it was then when I realized this was a bad idea. A very, very bad idea. My gaze skittered from one friend to the other. "You two better behave or else I am disowning you."

Brie took a sip of her wine, her eyes twinkling mischievously. "You should have thought about that before you made fun of my book the other day."

Lacy snort-laughed. "Was Brie reading about some Duke undoing the fair maiden's corset again."

"Hey!" Briana set her wine down and crossed her arms in front of her. "The two of you are going to swallow your words one of these days."

"There are better things to swallow, Brie."

There was a second of silence before laughter broke out around the table. And just like that, my two friends had all my nervousness dissipating.

"Either I missed the joke, or I *am* the joke."

Griffin's rich baritone filled the air surrounding us. I couldn't take my eyes off him as he placed the tray holding two beers and four shots on the table before he lowered his magnificent frame into the seat beside me. Cocking his head, his gaze traveled from my feet all the way to the top of my head. With a sinful smile playing on his lips, he grabbed my chair and pulled it closer to his.

He draped his arm over the back of my chair, his thumb drawing small circles on my shoulder. To Lacy, he said, "Forgive me, but you've had her way longer than I have."

Not even kidding, both of my friends swooned like freaking teenagers witnessing their first romantic moment. But who could blame them, everything this guy did was just so damn swoon-worthy.

"So, Griffin, tell me—" Brie leaned forward and immediately took on the role of lead reporter; questioning him about anything and everything she could think of.

With patience no man should possess, he listened and answered. Entertaining us with tales from his hometown, St. Mullins. Apparently, it was a little village situated in Carlow. Listening to him talk about his family with so much love and respect might've had me falling for him a little harder.

"Only the one brother, then?" Lacy inquired while sipping on her spritzer.

"That's right."

With her elbows on the table, she leaned forward, her chin resting on her folded hands. "He wouldn't happen to be single?" She playfully batted her lashes and pursed her lips.

Griffin chuckled and tugged me closer. "Collin is… complicated."

"Aren't all the good ones, though?" Brie mumbled around her wine glass. That nagging feeling that something was up with her and Thatcher took hold of me again. And for the first time in my life, I wanted to be that friend who meddled and pushed until she had all the answers.

"Refill anyone?" Griffin pushed his chair back. He was in the process of standing up when Lacy motioned for him to sit back down.

"Brie and I will get the drinks."

"I don't mind." He was still standing.

"Neither do I," was Lacy's reply. "Especially when the barman is as yummy-looking as that one. Come on." Without waiting she grabbed Brie's hand, and all but dragged our friend from the table. Before they disappeared into the crowd, I heard Brie say, "You know he's gay, right?"

With a chuckle Griffin sat back down, positioning himself so his legs were on either side of my chair. He ran his fingers along my arm, from my elbow to my shoulder. Tiny zips of electricity skittered across my skin. He curled his fingers around my nape, brushing his thumb along my jaw.

"I like your friends." That wasn't supposed to sound sexy or cause a tug in my belly and yet, that's exactly what happened.

"I think they like you too." *Why do I sound so breathless?*

With his free hand, he squeezed my knee before dragging his palm up and up. My heart rate kicked up a notch when his hand continued its journey upward, disappearing beneath my dress. Breathing became near impossible when he leaned forward and whispered, "Do you think they'd mind if I steal you away now?"

I sucked in my bottom lip when his darkened gaze collided with mine. "I don—"

"You have got to be kidding me."

If anything could burst my little lust-bubble, it was the sound of my brother's voice. Clearly, it had the same effect on Griffin because his fingers dug into my neck and thigh. His jaw was set, and his eyes trained on me. I shifted my gaze to the side to see Thatcher, Nathan and a few other guys standing behind Griffin. This time my pulse kicked into high gear for an entirely different reason. "Really Rae? *He* is the guy you told me about?"

"Thatch—"

Before I could even get a word in, Griffin jumped up. Shoulders squared, legs spread, he looked just as intimidating as Thatch even though my brother was a bit taller and wider. "You have a problem with that, Brooks?" The measured sound of every word had ice running through my veins.

"Damn right I have a problem," My brother spat back. "I don't want you near my sister."

This time I jumped up. "Don't I have a say in this?"

"She deserves someone way better than you, *Gallagher*."

It was as if I hadn't even said a word. I moved to stand between them, but Nathan grabbed my arm. "Maybe it's best to let them sort out their... issues here instead of at the station."

My gaze snapped to the two men in my life who looked ready to rip each other's heads off. Yanking my arm free, I shook my head, "No!"

I pushed between Thatcher and Griffin and being as short as I was, I looked like a dwarf towered by giants. With my arms spread wide, I yelled, "Hey!"

"This doesn't concern you." My idiot-brother had the audacity to push me out of the way.

I looked at Griffin and if murder hadn't been on his mind earlier, it sure as hell was now. He lunged forward and grabbed Thatcher by the shirt. "Don't you dare touch her."

"Go ahead," Thatcher bated. "Hit me. We'll see how highly Chief Abbott still thinks of you then."

My breath was trapped in my lungs. For a second, I was certain Griffin was going to punch my brother. A sigh of relief rushed over my lips when he let him go with the words, "You're not worth it."

His eyes found me and whatever he saw in mine made him wince. I stood rooted to the spot as he slowly approached me. When he reached forward and tucked a strand of hair behind my ear, I noticed that his fingers were trembling. "I think it's time for me to go." I took his hand in mine and glared at my brother while I said, "We're both leaving." Squeezing the hand in mine, I turned my attention to Griffin. "I'm going to say goodbye to Lacy and Brie, I'll meet you at the truck."

The question in his eyes was clear as day, and the answer was: No, I wasn't sure what I was doing. Just then my two friends pushed through the crowd, babbling and laughing. The smiles on their lips faded the moment they spotted us.

"You're sure?" Griffin's words were just for me.

My gaze roamed over his face, looking for an answer. I found it in the eyes boring into me. "Yes." He glanced at my brother before looking at me again. With a quick nod, he turned on his heels and headed for the exit.

I waited until I knew he was out of earshot before I turned to Thatcher. "You have no right!"

He glared down his nose at me, "You're making a mistake."

"So?" I threw my arms in the air. "It's my mistake to make."

"He's going to hurt you."

My lips pulled into a thin line while I shook my head. "How do you know? You don't even know him."

That vein in my brother's neck bulged again. "Neither do you!" His voice boomed through the crowded space. "You always do this, Rae! Always. And who is left picking up the pieces?"

If he'd laid a hand on me it would've hurt less than his words had. Furiously, I blinked away the tears that stung the back of my eyes.

"That's enough, Thatcher."

So entangled in my own emotions, I didn't even see Brie sidle up to Thatch nor did I see her place her hand on his arm. He looked down at the spot she was touching and then at her face. I was confused when I saw him wince in the same way Griffin had when he'd noticed me earlier.

Warm hands cupped my shoulders right before Lacy's whispered words reached my ears, "I'm not sure what we missed, but I think Brie just created an opportunity for you to leave." Judging by the way my friend and my brother were still staring at each other, I'd say it was a lot more than a diversion.

Whatever it was, I took it. I said a quick goodbye to Lacy before I rushed toward the exit. All the while praying that I was doing the right thing.

15

GRIFFIN

"Shite!" I ground me teeth and cursed some more. "Shite, shite, shite."

I knew better than to lose me temper in a public place, but when that idiot pushed Rae out of the way, common sense took a hike.

I dragged a frustrated hand through me hair before me palm smacked down on the hood of me truck.

"Dammit!"

This wasn't how tonight was supposed to go. Fingers spread, I placed both hands on the smooth surface of the hood. Me chin dropped to me chest and a heavy sigh blew over me lips. I had no clue where to go from here.

I liked Raelyn. A lot. But after that little stunt in the bar, it was clear her brother wasn't going to make things easy for us. As much as I was willing to fight for this girl, I wasn't prepared for her to go against her family.

As if merely thinking about her was enough to conjure her up, Rae appeared by me side. The sad look on her face piercing me heart. There was something very wrong with seeing me beautiful carefree Rae looking so troubled.

I reached for her and when she came without hesitancy, I released a breath I had no idea I was holding. Wrapping me arms around her, I held her as close as I could without crushing her.

"I'm sorry." We spoke at the same time.

Bringing me hands up to cup her shoulders, I gently pushed her back. Trapping her gaze with mine, I said, "There's no need for you to apologize. You didn't do anything wrong."

Rae nervously looked over her shoulder at the entrance of the bar. Her bottom lip wobbled just a bit, and she quickly rolled it over her teeth. I hated this. I wanted to curse some more. I wanted to storm back inside and ram me fist into Thatcher Brooks' face.

But what I wanted most was for that sad look on Rae's face to go away.

Taking her chin between me fingers, I guided her gaze back to mine. "You're sure you want to leave?"

She took a deep breath; her chest slowly rising and falling with the action. "Yes."

We climbed into the truck and a few minutes later I pulled out of the lot. The journey back to Donald's house was made in silence, and it wasn't the comfortable type either. It was obvious that the incident at the bar was weighing on Rae—as it should.

After rolling to a stop in the driveway, I switched off the ignition. Neither of us moved to get out, though. I looked over at Rae who was staring at her hands in her lap and hated myself for being part of the reason her smile was gone.

Reaching over, I curled me fingers around the back of her neck, me thumb brushing along her jaw. "I'm sorry your night is ruined."

"My night is not ruined," she said. I wasn't entirely sure if she was trying to convince me or herself. "I'm just disappointed that Thatcher refuses to see past his own stubbornness."

"Your brother…" I shook me head. "*Cic maith se tóin atá dlíth air*. The bloody *cúl tóna* needs to mind his own damn business."

Rae pulled away from me touch. Her back ramrod straight. "Yes, I agree, Thatch probably is whatever name you just called him but," she took a sharp breath. "he's still *my* brother. And I don't want you insulting him to my face."

She was right. He was her family and right now I was the guy shoving a wedge between them. Shite, that was the last thing I wanted. "Of course. I'm sorry."

Angling me head away from her, I stared at the darkness outside. "You should go make things right with him. And you should do it now."

"What are you saying?"

Shifting me gaze back to Rae, I forced the words out. "You shouldn't be here with me until you make things right with your brother. Nothing and no one should ever be more important than family."

She gave me a look that might as well have been a punch to the gut. "Right… you don't want me here. Got it." There was no mistaking the current of hurt running through her words. Tugging on the handle, she had her door open before I could utter another word.

By the time I got out of the truck, she was already halfway to her car parked in front of the house. Breaking into a jog, I caught up with her and curled me fingers around her arm. "Rae, wait. I didn't mean it like that."

"I think you've made it perfectly clear where we stand. Me hand slid down and wrapped around hers. "Don't leave like this."

She cast her gaze to the sky, her shoulders rising and falling with an exasperated sigh "I'm confused. Maybe jumping into this without giving it a second thought wasn't the best idea."

I couldn't blame her for thinking that when the same thoughts had been running through me mind as well. However, just the thought that she might leave and never come back had me breaking out in a cold sweat. "Rae, please?"

She placed her free hand on top of mine and pried me fingers loose. "Good night, Griffin." Taking two steps backward, she spun around and marched to her car. As I watched her taillights disappear into the darkness, I couldn't help but think I'd lost her before I really even had her.

16

RAELYN

Life was a rollercoaster ride.

One moment, you're up, sitting on top of the world feeling untouchable. The next, you're crashing to the ground at high speed. I needed to take my frustration out on something, anything. Preferably a six-foot-something idiot who shared my last name.

He wasn't in the vicinity, but unfortunately, my car door was. And so was the front door and the kitchen cupboards. Scouring the kitchen for Thatcher's whiskey, I opened and slammed door after door until I finally found the alcohol in the cupboard where we kept the pots and pans.

Grabbing a tumbler from the dry-rack by the sink, I poured myself a good three fingers worth of the liquid. Bringing it to my lips, I carefully sampled the contents of the glass. The moment the taste hit my tongue, everything went spraying out of my mouth.

"Ugh, that's disgusting." I groaned and immediately stuck my tongue in and out of my mouth in an attempt to get rid of the horrible taste that still lingered there. After I poured the whiskey down the drain, I grabbed an orange juice from the fridge and almost moaned when the citrusy tang hit my taste buds.

When my thirst was satisfied and just the zesty taste of oranges left on my tongue, I screwed the cap back on and slumped into the nearest seat. I cradled my head in my hands all the while wondering where the hell everything took a left turn.

As much as I wished it could, replaying the night's events over and over again didn't offer up any answers. In fact, it left me with more questions. I dragged my hand through my hair, my gaze turning toward the ceiling.

"Men," I grunted on a heavy sigh. I swear there wasn't a single one alive who knew what they wanted. And then they have the audacity to say us woman are complicated. Please! Give me a break.

I knew what, or rather who, I wanted. But apparently his thoughts on family values outranked me. And the more I thought about it, the more furious I got. At Griffin. At Thatcher. Because neither of them even took a moment to ask me what the hell I wanted.

"Ughhh!"

All this going in circles was hurting my damn brain. Slipping off the stool, I headed for my bedroom, flicking off the kitchen light on my way out. After I got a sleep shirt from my drawer, I stripped down to my underwear and pulled the soft cotton over my head.

Barefoot, I padded to the bathroom to wash my face and brush my teeth. I bent over the sink to rinse my mouth a final time and when I came up my brother's reflection scared the life out of me. For an over-sized jerk, he sure moved around silently. "What the hell?"

"Didn't think I'd find you here."

With the amount of eye-rolling Thatcher was causing me to do, I feared I was turning into a teenager. "It's my house too, where else would I be?"

My brother pulled a face that made his disgust clear. "With *him*."

"Oh come off of it, Thatch." I planted my hands on my hips and glared at him. "You're being unreasonable."

"This town is full of decent, hard-working men who'd give their left nut to be with you, why did you have to pick him."

Shaking my head, I pushed past him and made my way to my room. I knew he'd be short on my heels. "Are you even listening to yourself?" I asked. "Do you honestly believe I saw him and thought: *Oh look, it's the guy my brother hates, I think I'll date him*?"

Pivoting, I found Thatch standing in the doorway. With his brows drawn together and deep creases marring his forehead, I knew he was stewing on my words.

I took the opportunity while his defenses were down. "I get why you don't like the guy, I really do. But did you ever stop to think about me? *I* like him, Thatch."

"Rae, I don't know what to tell you, this guy just rubs me the wrong way."

Tiredness seeped into my bones, I lowered myself onto the edge of the bed. "If he wasn't the guy who took the job you wanted, you wouldn't be feeling this way." It was time for some hard truths I knew he didn't want to hear. "Have you ever taken a minute and really thought about why you've been passed over so many times?"

His jaw started ticking. "You like doing things *your* way, regardless of what rule you're breaking."

A strangled sound came from the back of his throat, "It wasn't enough that the bastard came into my town and took my job, he had to take my sister too."

"See? This is what I'm talking about. You don't listen, Thatch." Heaviness crept into my heart. "I'm tired. Can we not do this now?"

Thatcher stepped into the room and sat down on the bed next to me, his hand on my knee. "I'm not saying the right things, am I?"

I shifted so I could look into his eyes. "I don't need you to say the right things, I need you to hear me when I talk." My hand found his, and I held it tight. "I love you, Thatch. But you have to understand that I am a grown woman who needs to make her own decisions.

You can't protect me from everything, even though I know you want to."

"If I don't look out for you, who will?"

Shaking my head, I stared at the carpet. Thatch would never surrender his role as protector, I could only hope that we would find common ground on the subject. "I appreciate you always having my back, but do you think that you can step back a bit while I figure out where this thing with Griffin is going?"

The mention of his name had my brother's jaw ticking away again. "I don't like him."

"But I do, Thatch. A lot."

As my brother's eyes roamed over my face, I noticed how troubled he looked. "If he hurts you…"

I patted his hand, "I know, you'll kill him." I hoped adding a wink would break the tension between us. Fighting with Thatch was never fun.

"I can't promise anything," he said as he pushed to his feet. "But I'll try." He bent down and dropped a kiss to my head. "Just promise me you'll keep both eyes open."

"Always."

Long after Thatch had left my room, I still sat in the same spot. My mind replayed everything from the moment I'd met Griffin up until I drove away from him. I knew what I was feeling was crazy, but it didn't make the feelings go away. It didn't make me want to explore things with him any less either.

The sound of my phone dinging somewhere finally pulled me out of my stupor. Getting to my feet, I snatched it from the dresser. My notification bar showed I had three unread messages. With a swipe of my thumb, I unlocked the screen to read them.

Griffin: *I'm sorry.*

Griffin: *Rae*?

Griffin: *I'm coming over*.

17

GRIFFIN

Me intentions had been good but leaving things with Rae like this felt all sorts of wrong. I'd known I'd made a mistake the very moment she got in her car and drove off. I'd been a coward because I didn't want any more guilt on me shoulders.

But all the guilt in the world couldn't possibly feel as heavy as me heart did right now. Me words had hurt her, and I needed to make it right.

Heading back to me truck, I fired off a few messages before dialing Nathan's number. He answered just as I slid behind the wheel. "Nathan, I need Brooks' address."

There was a long pause. "Are you sure that's a good idea? He's pretty pissed off."

"He can be as pissed as he wants to be," I growled into the phone. "It's not him I care about."

He chuckled softly. "Well all right but don't say I didn't warn you. Do you have a pen?"

Grabbing whatever I could find, I wrote as fast as Nathan spoke. "Appreciate it, man." Not even bothering with disconnecting the call, I dropped the phone in me lap and turned the key in the ignition. Five minutes later, I was parked in front of the address I'd scribbled on the back of a gas station receipt. Tilting me head, I stared at the house beyond the window.

Even though it was nighttime, the little solar lights strategically placed in the flower beds illuminated the yard with pops of color. I was certain if I stepped on the lawn with me bare feet, they'd sink away in the lush looking green carpet.

Me gaze shifted from the yard to the inky colored door. Was she in there waiting for me? Swiping me phone to life, I stared at the message thread between me and Rae. She'd read me messages but still hadn't responded. That had me feeling all sorts of things. None of them pleasant.

For a second, I contemplated not going in at all. If Thatcher were to answer the door, we'd have another showdown, no doubt. Then the organ inside me chest reminded me that Rae was a girl worth fighting for— even if it was her brother I needed to fight.

Determined, I stepped out of me truck and approached the house. The sound of the gate creaking sliced through the still of the night. I hurried along the cobblestone path and took the stairs that led to the door two at a time.

Drawing in a breath, I tapped me knuckles against the wood two times. Then I waited… and waited… and waited. Just as I brought me hand up to knock again, the door slowly opened a crack revealing only half of the woman I came to see.

It bugged me that she felt the need to keep the door as a barrier between us.

"Can I come in?"

Rae chewed on her cheek and looked over her shoulder at something in the house. "Thatch is here," she stated when her gaze found mine again.

"I didn't come to see him. I came to see you." I dragged me palm over me face. "To apologize. To explain." She studied me with guarded eyes but said nothing. "Please, Rae?"

Finally, she moved to the side and opened the door wide. I stepped inside but instead of venturing further into the house, I turned to face Rae. I couldn't explain why I did what I did. Maybe it was the way she was staring at me with her eyes taking up half of her face. Or maybe it was the way she rolled her lip between her teeth.

Or maybe it was just because I wanted to.

I took a step closer. Cradling her cheeks between me palms, I lowered me mouth to hers. I kissed her hard, conveying everything I felt but had no idea how to voice.

And Rae… well, she kissed me right back.

She nibbled on me lip, pulling one of those unholy hisses from the back of me throat before she tore her mouth away from mine. "This is not how explaining works."

I pushed me hand into her hair and brought her lips back to mine. "No," I said into her mouth. "It's not." Unable to help myself, I kissed her again. This time, however, it was slow and deep causing a myriad of emotions to riot within me.

When I pulled back and saw her flushed cheeks and heavy lids, it took all me restraint not to dive back in and sample her sweet mouth. But I didn't come here for that. I dragged me fingers through her hair before I tucked a few strands behind her ear. "Can we sit somewhere?"

She sobered instantly; those walls back up. With a nod, she indicated for me to follow her. If only she knew I'd follow her to the ends of the damn earth.

A few silent moments later, we entered a kitchen that looked as homey as the one at Donald's place. The one where Rae and I shared kisses. Made breakfast together. Where I realized exactly how fast I was falling.

"Do you want something to drink?" Rae's soft question drew me attention back to her.

I cleared me throat. "Water's fine, thank you."

After pulling a water and an orange juice from the fridge, she motioned toward the breakfast nook. "We can sit there." I slipped onto one of the stools and me heart sank when Rae dragged the other one around, putting the island between us.

She handed me the water and picked at the label of her juice, quietly waiting for me. But as I sat there looking at her, I wasn't quite sure where or even how to start. Those beautiful eyes of hers lifted to mine and as always knocked the breath right out of me lungs. I realized she deserved nothing less than me truth. "I never thought I'd leave Sault Point; it was me home. I care for the people there as much as I care for me family back in Ireland."

I unscrewed the cap of the bottle and took a few swallows. Alcohol would've gone better with what I was about to tell her. "You already know about me blood-related brother, you don't know about Adam, though. We don't share the same DNA but he's me brother too. I've known him for ten years. I was the best man at his wedding and his right hand at the station."

Knowing what was coming next, I had to swallow down the pain that lodged itself in me throat. "I have never seen a better firefighter than Adam, he had this ability to keep calm in the worst situations.

Unfortunately, when it comes to people you love, your common sense goes out the window."

I knew she wanted the barrier between us. The thing was I needed her to ground me. I only realized it when I reached across the counter and took her hand in mine. The moment I touched her, some of the heaviness on me shoulders lifted.

"I had no clue a stupid gas leak would cause so much pain." I closed me eyes for a second as the events of that night replayed in me mind. The crying, the screaming, the flames. They were all so vivid, I might as well have been standing in Adam's house.

"Griffin?" Like the lifeline she'd become in this short period she'd been in me life, Rae's sweet voice pulled me from the depths of me very own hell. Her blue eyes, me saving grace.

Me gaze traveled to our connected hands and then to the counter between us. I jumped up so fast I startled her. "Sorry," I mumbled while I gripped the chair and dragged it to her side. When we sat facing each other, our knees pressed together, I took both her hands in mine.

"Adam lost his wife in a housefire. He tried to save her but ended up hurt really bad. When he came out of the hospital, the Adam I knew wasn't there anymore. Me best friend—me brother—was gone. He died with Angie that day."

"That's awful." Her voice was soft and soothing.

"Aye, 'tis. So is what I did." Me gaze flitted to the opening that led into the kitchen just to make sure we were alone. "See, Adam blames me for what happened. He thinks I stopped searching for Angie to pull him out." I swallowed hard. "It's a heavy burden to carry, even though logically I understand there was nothing I could've done.

"I guess sometimes it's just easier to believe the bad instead of the good, you know? So when Adam placed the blame on me shoulders, I took it. But it made facing his family every day even harder. Because in the back of me mind I always wondered if they blamed me too."

Me tongue slicked over me dry lips. "Eventually it got so bad, I couldn't go to the store without wondering who else blamed me for Angie's death. It became too much. I felt myself slip into this big black hole and I knew I had to do something.

"I'd gotten to know Donald while he was in Sault Point to train the probies and he'd gone out on a few runs with us while he was there. The last time I'd seen him, he'd offered me a job. When I declined, he told me the offer would always be there."

Rae's eyes lit up with understanding. "Donald knows a good firefighter when he sees one."

"Maybe. But I upended an entire house just because I couldn't deal with me shite."

She cocked her head to the side, "Don't you think you deserve the space and time to heal on your own? Sometimes doing what's best for us may seem selfish to others, that doesn't mean we shouldn't do it." Rae pulled her hand from mine to press her palm against me cheek. "It's okay to put your needs first. If you can't take care of yourself, how are you going to take care of others?"

In that moment I realized that fate was a very real thing. It brought me her. I had no words to express how I felt, so I did the only thing I could. Surging forward, I pressed me mouth to hers. I took and took and took, kissing her as if her lips were the only thing keeping me sane. They probably were.

I felt her shift and before I could properly gather me thoughts, Rae was straddling me lap. Her hips flexed, drawing a deep groan from the back of me throat. It took a lot of effort, but I managed to tear me mouth from hers. I had no idea how me hands had ended up in her hair, but I took the opportunity to pull her forehead to mine.

"Nothing compares to making love to you, acushla. But tonight, I just want to hold you, and tomorrow I want to wake up with you next to me."

I wasn't sure what I expected, but it sure as hell wasn't Rae slipping off me lap and guiding me to her bedroom. In the center of her room, I stood rooted to the spot while she shut the door and padded back to me. Her blue eyes piercing through me as she gripped the hem of me shirt and pulled it up. When she pushed it as far as she could, I took over and pulled it over me head. I bit down on me teeth and dragged in a breath through me nose when her fingers went to work on me jeans.

When all that was left were me briefs, Rae brought her mouth to me chest, placing a tender kiss there before pushing onto her toes to press her lips against me jaw. "Then hold me."

***

Something tickled me nose, and it didn't matter which way I scrunched it, the feeling wouldn't go away. I popped one eye open and immediately smiled when a mass of brown hair blurred me vision. By the steady sound of her breathing, I could tell she was fast asleep. Her back was pressed against me chest and me arm banded around her waist.

Waking up like this had a weird sense of calm spreading through me. It also had me wishing I could wake up like this every day. With that thought I

abruptly pushed into a seated position. As much as I
cared for Adam and Angie, I'd always envied them a
little. It was a rare thing to find that one person who,
no matter how much they infuriated you, you couldn't
imagine waking up without them.

I had never felt that way about someone.

Not once.

Until now.

I looked down at Rae's sleeping form. How much I
had come to care for this woman in such a short period
of time should have scared the shite out of me. But it
didn't. It felt right and natural. Not being able to resist
feeling her skin beneath me fingertips, I brushed them
over her cheek. She stirred but didn't wake.

With me smile still firmly in place, I slipped out from
beneath the covers. I snatched me jeans from the floor
and after pulling them on, headed for the kitchen.

Scavenging for me morning coffee was becoming part
of me daily routine. I'd just triumphantly pressed the
button on the machine when I heard shuffling.

I spun around expecting to find Rae looking all sorts of
sexy in that little sleep shirt of hers. Yeah, I didn't find
that. Instead, Thatcher stood in the opening, a
murderous look flashing in his eyes.

"You spent the night?" His gritted-out words sounded
a lot like: *Did you screw my sister under my roof?*

Squaring me shoulders, I widened me stance. "I needed to see Rae."

His jaw muscle started jumping, his nostrils flaring with the effort it took to not lose his shite. "It had to be *you*," he mumbled with a shake of his head.

"Look man, you and I will probably always have our shite. I'm good with that. But I'm not prepared to walk away from whatever this is just because you can't stand the sight of me."

A strangled sound came from the back of his throat as he stalked toward the fridge. He yanked it open and pulled milk, eggs and cheese from it. After placing everything on the counter, he planted his palms on the surface and aimed a glare me way.

"She's not just my sister, she's the most important thing in my life." With a heavy sigh, he cocked his head toward the opening before looking at me again.

"She's had enough hurt to last her two lifetimes, if you add to that… so help me…"

Said a lot about a man's character when he was willing to do anything to protect his family. In that moment, I had a lot of respect for Thatcher Brooks. I wasn't stupid, the pissing contest between the two of us was far from over, but where Rae was concerned, we could at least try to be civil.

"Everything okay in here?"

Me gaze flicked to the entrance of the kitchen where Rae stood. Her hair tumbling over her shoulder and her beautiful face etched with worry. Those eyes of hers flitted between me and her brother while her teeth worried her lip.

"All good," Thatcher said. When I looked at him, he added, "We have an understanding."

Me eyes found Rae's again and I couldn't help but smile at the woman who'd stolen me heart. "We do," I confirmed.

Her shoulders immediately relaxed. "Oh good." Relief evident in her voice. She rushed toward me and wrapped her arms around me waist. Tilting her head back, she beamed up at me. I couldn't resist, I bent down and took the kiss I'd been craving since me eyes opened.

"Ugh, I don't need to see this."

Even with Thatcher's protest, I couldn't bring myself to tear me lips away from me girl. *Me girl*. Man, did I like the sound of that.

Now that Raelyn Brooks was mine, there was no way I was letting her go.

18

RAELYN

"Wakey wakey, sleepy head."

I groaned and snuggled deeper into Griffin's chest. His deep chuckle vibrated through my body and filled the room.

"You have to get up, acushla, we need to leave soon." Tilting my head back, I cracked one eye open and peeked up at him. I didn't think I'd ever get tired of looking at his ruggedly handsome face first thing in the morning. His eyes were soft. His mouth relaxed. And the scruff covering his face a few shades darker.

Mmm, I bet the scrape of those whiskers would feel amazing against my skin. Especially when—

"I know what you're thinking." He lowered his head, eyes dancing wickedly. "There's no time. We have a three-hour drive ahead of us."

Scrunching up my nose, I leaned my forehead against his chest again. "Ah boo, you're no fun."

His fingers swept up my leg, brushing over my hipbone. "That's not what you said last night." He shifted his big body, and I grinned victoriously at what I felt trapped between us. "Maybe you forgot?"

"Yes," I said sweetly. "I don't remember a thing."

In a flash I was flat on my back with him hovering over me. Griffin braced his thick forearms on either side of my head, his body unbelievably still. Dark, dark eyes boring into mine, promising sinfully delicious things.

I wanted those things. So badly.

Arching my back, I pushed my breasts against his chest and almost moaned at the feeling of his bristly hair scraping my sensitive skin. His jaw wasn't the only thing that turned hard as granite, and yet he didn't move an inch.

Smiling sweetly, I lifted my head and slicked my tongue over his lips, the tip barely slipping inside. His chest vibrated with the growl he wanted to set free, but still he remained steady. I nibbled on his lip, his jaw, he did nothing.

Which was unfortunate because all this teasing was pushing me way beyond the point of being turned-on. Way, way beyond. And if he didn't do something soon, I feared I might die. *Here lies Raelyn Brooks. Age twenty-two. Cause of Death: Sexual frustration.*

Before that could happen, I reached between us and closed my hand around him. I almost let out a victory cry when he hissed his pleasure and pushed his hips forward. Lowering his head, he bared his teeth in a grin that was so freaking hot if I'd been wearing any clothes they would've melted right off.

"You don't play fair," he groaned against my mouth as I continued my slow and steady torture. One, two pumps and he yanked my hand away, pinning both above my head. There was no time to protest because his mouth was on mine barely a breath later.

He kissed me long and hard. Then moved to deep and slow. He kissed me like he was memorizing every stroke of my tongue. Like he couldn't get enough. Like I was his, and he was mine.

Tilting his head, he sucked on my bottom lip before trailing a line of wet kisses from my jaw to my ear. His mouth moved down my neck, nipping and sucking as he went. As wonderful as it was, I needed more. I needed him to fill me.

Complete me.

"Griffin," I moaned breathlessly. "Please."

He lifted his head; what I saw shining in those dark irises stole my breath. Once, twice he brushed his mouth over mine. "You and me, Rae," he groaned. "You and me."

"Yes." Just as the word rolled off my tongue, Griffin pushed my knee to my chest and snapped his hips forward. I almost whimpered. His big hands shot to my thighs, fingers finding skin. I speared my fingers through his hair, digging the tips into the back of his head.

I moaned. He grunted. Together we moved at an agonizingly slow pace that only seemed to heighten the pleasure. With every roll of his hips, he pushed me closer and closer to the edge. Until my body finally, *finally*, fell apart in an earth-shattering explosion that I felt all the way to the center of my heart.

I was still riding the waves of pleasure when Griffin shouted my name and dropped his head to my clammy shoulder. My hand raked through his damp hair, my smile lazy. "Mhm, so good."

His lips touched the spot below my ear. "You're a distraction, acushla." Another kiss. "Now come on, get that sexy little arse of yours in the shower because we need to leave."

***

My gaze shifted from the rolling scenery beyond the window to the man sitting beside me. Eyes focused on the road, jaw set, he held the steering wheel in a white-knuckled grip. I reached over the center console and placed my hand on his thigh.

"Stop stressing. Everything is going to be fine." A bold statement to make since I didn't know that for a fact. But honestly, I could hardly see today going bad. From the bits Griffin had told me about them, I was positive Mr. and Mrs. Carlisle were looking forward to seeing him.

On the other hand, I understood Griffin's hesitancy too. It couldn't be easy walking around with the kind of guilt that made you think you needed to do more to save someone's life.

The warmth of his hand on mine when he gave it a small squeeze pulled me from my thoughts. He gave me a quick glance and one of those smiles that said *look, I'm pretending to be just fine.*

I wanted to tell him again that everything was going to be all right when he tapped his indicator and we turned left into a long driveway. The truck slowly rolled to a stop, the engine going silent a few seconds later.

Silence filled the cab as Griffin stared at the little porch dotted with colourful flowerpots. In that moment, I would've given anything to take whatever bad feeling he was feeling. I'd keep it, carry it, if it meant he didn't have to.

His eyes shot to mine. "I can't do this."

"Yes, you can." I reached for his hand on the steering wheel. After prying it lose, I took it in mine. "You can do this because it's what you need."

A deep line formed on his forehead. "I don't want to see how much I disappointed them."

Squeezing his fingers, I promised, "Whatever happens, I'm here and I'm not going anywhere."

Griffin's hand shot out, fingers hooking around the back of my neck, pulling my face to his. He kissed me hard, verging on the edge of being painful. But if that was what he needed to get through today, I'd give it ten times over.

When we pulled apart, he leaned his forehead against mine. "Thank you." The kiss he gave me after that was so sweet, so achingly sweet I felt it in the deepest, darkest corners of my soul.

We got out of the truck, Griffin immediately wrapping his fingers around mine as we took the steps and approached the front door. He gave me a long meaningful glance before lifting his hand to tap his knuckles against the wood.

I swear, I could feel the pulse of his nervous energy seep into my pores and I hated it for him. I held on tighter to his hand and even though we were standing next to each other, I snuggled closer still.

I was about to reassure him one last time when the door suddenly flew open and a body came flying toward us. "Griffin," the lady cooed. Her voice wistful and cheery as if her long lost son had finally returned.

"Hello Mildred."

The words were barely out of his mouth when she squeezed his cheeks between her palms and pressed loud smacking kisses wherever she found a spot. Griffin screwed his eyes shut and scrunched up his nose.

He looked so freaking adorable that a small laugh bubbled over my lips before I could check it. The little lady's assault on my boyfriend stopped, her eyes zeroing in on me. "And who is this?"

Her smile was so big and wide, it made me feel warm all over. "Rae." I pulled my hand from Griffin's and held it out to her. "So nice to meet you, Mrs. Carlisle." Her gaze flicked to my hand, studying it for a long second before she swatted it away and crushed me to her chest. Pretty sure I looked like a deer caught in headlights for the few moments it took me to recover and hug her back.

"Come in, come in."

Mrs. Carlisle shuffled us inside where I found out her husband's hugs were even more fierce than his wife's. But I didn't mind. Especially not when I spotted the relief so evident on Griffin's face.

Once we were settled with a glass of homemade lemonade, Mrs. Carlisle balanced on the edge of the couch. Knees tightly pressed together, hands resting in her lap, she looked at the man beside me with so much wonder it just about melted my heart.

"Tell me everything," she begged. "Do you like the new town? And the station?"

Griffin's gaze shot to me, his lips lifting in one corner.
"I love it." The butterflies in my tummy went freaking
loopy as his focus returned to Mrs. Carlisle. "As for
the station… it's been hard, as you can imagine.
Change is never easy but I'm confident we'll catch our
stride soon."

His tongue glided over his lips, his Adam's apple
slowly bobbing up and down. "How's Adam holding
up?" Mrs. Carlisle hung her head, her husband
immediately reaching for her hand. "I'm sorry,"
Griffin said quickly.

Her gray head moved side to side as she shook it
tentatively. "Don't apologize." She pinned him with a
stare so serious I felt the effect of it. "It's not your
fault."

Beside me, Griffin heaved out a shaky breath. "I know,
but—"

"No buts, Griffin." Her voice was sharp. Determined.
"What happened breaks my heart every day. It's not
right. It's not fair. But it sure as hell isn't your fault
either." She was on her feet and in front of him within
the space of a breath. Pulling him to her, she pleaded,
"Stop doing this to yourself."

His entire body shuddered, arms going around Mrs.
Carlisle. "Aye."

My eyes burned a little as the enormity of the moment
settled around us. This was what he needed. For

someone—no, not just someone, for *them*—to assure him he'd done nothing wrong.

When they finally pulled apart, Griffin slung his arm over my shoulder and tugged me close to him.

Everything after that was just wonderful. They caught up while I learned more about the man who'd stolen my heart.

We laughed until we cried.

Then we cried when we flipped through photo albums. Then we laughed some more.

By the time we disappeared into the guestroom on the second floor, my cheeks ached, and my heart felt full. So incredibly full. I was still smiling when Griffin came to a standstill in front of me. Gently, he took my face in his hands, eyes roaming over my features. "I couldn't have done this without you."

I swallowed thickly at the sincerity in his voice. "Of course you could."

He inched closer, lips brushing mine with every word he whispered, "I'm glad I didn't have to. You mean a lot to me, Rae. Hell, I think I might even—" his chest expanded with the sudden deep breath he needed.

But I got it.

Because I kinda sorta loved him too.

19

GRIFFIN

"Just one more kiss."

I grabbed Rae by the wrist, tugging her back to me before she had time to get into her car.

"Seriously, I'm going to—" Her little protest dissolved into nothingness the moment I slanted me mouth over hers. A happy sigh blew over her lips and settled somewhere inside me heart.

"Mhmmm." She drew back, peering up at me through thick lashes. "What was I saying again?"

Me hands gripped her hips. "That we should just skip work and go back to bed."

"You're bad."

I nipped at her neck. "But you love it."

Laughing, Rae pushed at me chest. "We're going to be terribly late if you keep this up."

"Fine," I said. Me tone over-dramatic as I took a step out of her personal space. "Text me when you get to work so I know you're safe."

She waved me off. "Stop it. The Home is ten minutes away. Nothing bad is going to happen between now and then."

I was about to tell her otherwise when she pushed onto her toes and stole the words from me tongue. When I moved to deepen the kiss, she pulled back and quickly hopped into her Mazda.

With a sharp shake of me head, I braced me hands on me hips. "Little minx. You're so going to pay for that."

Rae's lips twitched as she turned the key in the ignition. Once her engine sputtered to life, she turned to me; her eyes raking over me body in a way that left no doubt as to what she was thinking. "I'm counting on it."

And then she was gone. Pulling out of the driveway, leaving me to stare at her disappearing taillights with a stupid grin on me face like some lovesick fool.

Which I definitely was.

I was still grinning like a damn idiot when I walked into the station fifteen minutes later. It finally felt as if life made a hell of a lot more sense. Like the anvil had been lifted from me chest and I could finally breathe easy again.

And Raelyn Brooks was at the center of it all.

***

"You guys have plans on Saturday?" Nathan asked from his spot in front of the stove. Usually when he was on breakfast duty, we could expect a decent spread of eggs, toast, bacon, and whatever the hell he could throw on the plate.

I was already salivating.

Coffee in hand, I parked me arse on the stool to the side of him. "No plans yet, why?"

"I just realized you were never properly welcomed to the team. Figured we should rectify that." He cracked the last two of what looked like two dozen eggs, beat them vigorously before dropping them into the warm pan. "George's parents have a nice piece of land not to far out of town, great spot for a big ole barbeque."

Something inside me shifted. That feeling of being home seeping into me bones. "I'll check with Rae, but I don't think there'll be a problem."

Nathan grinned. "Good."

Just then Brooks came ambling in. He jerked his head in greeting before grabbing a coffee and settling on one of the couches.

Nathan leaned forward. "What? No *my-dick-is-bigger-than-yours* today?"

Smiling into me coffee, I lifted me shoulder. "I think Brooks and I have finally come to some sort of understanding."

At least that's what I hoped. We weren't best buds suddenly. We didn't have beers together or say more to each other than was needed. But he hadn't stranded me anywhere again.

So, yeah, progress.

A weird sound came from the back of Nathan's throat. I wasn't sure if he was snorting or choking. Arching a brow, I pinned him with a stare. "What?"

His lips twitched as he continued to season the eggs with cracked black pepper. "You took his job. You're dating his sister. And he hasn't killed you yet. I think calling it an understanding is a severe understatement."

At the mention of her, I realized Rae never did text me to tell me she made it to work. I set me coffee down and reached for me phone, intending to give her a quick call to make sure she was all right.

I barely had time to scroll to her number when the firehouse alarm sounded. There was an odd sense of foreboding tapping against me ribs. A feeling that something horrible was about to happen. I quickly shoved it aside as we rushed to the change house to get into our gear.

When we got onto the rig and dispatch announced it was a fire call that feeling came back tenfold. Nervous energy licked its way down me spine. Me heart turned over inside me chest.

The last time I'd been at the scene of a fire was the night Adam lost Angie. A night I'd much rather forget. I looked at the men around me and although I only knew them for a short while, I had to believe they had me back. That we had each other's backs.

The radio crackled as the dispatcher rambled off the address where we were needed. In front of me Nathan and George blurted out, "Oh shit."

Me gaze bounced from one worried face to the next. "Oh shite, what?"

Nathan's worried stare flicked to Thatcher which had me looking at him too. There was no color in his cheeks and his fingers were curled around the steering wheel in a white-knuckled grip.

"Nathan, what the hell is going on?" I demanded.

Slowly his attention turned to me again. "That address," he said carefully, "It's where Raelyn works."

Oh shite no.

Panic curled a tight fist around me heart. *We are responding to a fire alarm at Rae's place of work.* I squeezed me eyes shut. *No, no, no. This can't be happening. I can't lose someone else like this. Not like this.*

By the time we pulled up in front of the old age home, a crowd had already gathered.

Me heart was beating fast. Too fast. Each frantic slam against me ribs so painful, I could hardly breathe.

I knew I needed to shift focus. Rae needed me and I'd be of no use to her if I lost me shite before I even made it off the rig.

Pulling in a deep breath through me nose, I held it for three seconds before slowly releasing it.

"Those people need to stay out of the way," I said to George once me feet hit the ground. "Handle it."

"On it." He jumped into action and headed toward the crowd.

I pointed at Nathan and the guy standing next to him. "We need to assess and contain immediately." With quick nods, they headed out too.

Thatcher got out from behind the wheel and I rushed over to him. His eyes looked wild, but I knew it was because he was worried. I felt it too. I flattened me palms against his chest. "You need to focus, Brooks." Gaze trained on the burning building—the building I had yet to look at—he didn't even acknowledge me.

"Are you listening to me, Thatcher? You need to focus!" I repeated. Louder this time. "Get your head in the game."

One broken word fell from his lips, "Rae."

Just hearing her name had panic surging through me veins. Me heart slammed harder. Faster. Me lungs felt tight and me feet itched with the need to sprint into that building to find Rae. *Me Rae.*

I finally understood why Adam had just bolted into the house that night and I understood his pain too. Because I didn't even know how bad the situation was and already a pain I hadn't known before shot through me. Completely paralyzing me.

Sucking in another breath, I tried to push it back as far as I possibly could. I needed to remain in control. And I needed this hot-head not to do something stupid.

I opened me mouth to tell Thatcher exactly that when I spotted Nathan rushing toward us. The look on his face locked the air in me lungs.

"Give me good news." I had no idea how I managed to speak past the burning in me throat.

Nathan eyed Thatcher wearily before he shook his head. "One of the employees said they got most of the residents out before the fire spread." He hesitated, his gaze flitting between me and Thatcher.

"Nathan! Spit it out!"

"Mr. Bishop never made it out and when she arrived Raelyn went in to find him."

"Shite."

Beneath me palm, Thatcher's body started to shake. I pushed harder into his chest. "Brooks, you're not going in there. I need you outside." I leveled him with a stare. "That's an order."

Anger, panic, and sadness flashed in his eyes. "Rae's in there."

I had to believe me own words when I vowed, "We'll
get her out." Shaking his head, he tried to push forward
but I shoved him back and yelled, "Listen to me!"
Softening me tone, I continued, "If you go in there, it's
one more body we have to worry about."

For a moment it looked as if understanding had
dawned but then he got a vacant look in his eyes.
"Screw you!"

His words were barely out before his fist connected
with me jaw. The moment I reared back, he set off
running toward the burning building.

20

GRIFFIN

"Shite!"

As much as I wanted to storm after Thatcher, I needed to be safe more. Barging into a burning building without protective gear was asking for trouble.

"I need you to take charge," I told Nathan just before I pulled on me oxygen mask. When he nodded, I spun on me heels and raced after Thatcher. He'd disobeyed a direct order, and in the process put not only his own life but the life of the people still trapped inside on the line too.

As furious as I was, I understood where his mind was at.

The building came closer and closer, me heart thrashing around like a wild animal. Cold claws of panic stabbed through me veins. Fear clutched an angry hand around me throat. Me chest felt tight. Me lungs hot.

I couldn't let it consume me.

I needed to be strong.

For Rae.

Forcing air in through me nose, I held it for four long seconds. Then released it at the same time as I sprinted through the open door. A thick blanket of smoke hung in the air, instantly clouding me vision.

Memories, dreadful memories flashed before me eyes, threatening to consume me. I blinked them away.

"Brooks!" No reply. "Rae!" Again, nothing. Me hand shook as I pressed the button on me radio and asked Nathan to get me directions to Mr. Bishop's room.

The further I ventured inside, though, the more panic clawed at me chest. Shite, I had to find them. Find her. Because this wasn't one of those fires that would be easily put out. I'd be surprised if the building was even salvageable after this.

A loud cracking sound sliced through the air. To me left a beam broke free from the ceiling and smashed to the ground.

"Thatcher!" This time faint coughing answered me call. "Brooks, where the hell are you?" I mumbled to myself as I strained to hear more sounds. I turned right, and the coughing grew louder and louder.

Then somehow through the haze I could faintly make out a pair of boots.

I rushed forward; panic seized me again when I found Thatcher slumped over in a coughing fit. Bending down, I grabbed his arm and threw it over me shoulder, me own arm supporting him around the waist. He was still coughing furiously when we started toward the exit.

"Did you find Rae?"

He shook his head. It took all me willpower not to tell him that the time it was taking me to get him out of the building was time I could've spent looking for his sister. When we reached the opening again, I was grateful to see Nathan already waiting, oxygen in hand.

"Make sure he stays put." I said to him when he took Thatcher from me. I didn't wait for his answer, I needed to find Rae.

More wood splintered to the ground while the fire kept crackling on. The fear inside me heart kept growing and growing as I entered room after room only to find it empty. Static filled me ears before Nathan's voice filtered through, "Griff, the chief wants you out. She is going to collapse."

No, no, no.

I didn't answer him, instead, I picked up me pace. I heard more splintering and looked up just in time to see a beam head straight toward me. Diving forward, I managed to avoid the falling piece of wood.

"Gallagher." It was Chief Abbott this time. "I understand why you feel you have to be in there now, but son, this building is coming down. I want you out." I closed me eyes for a second. Hissing, creaking, and crackling filled me ears. Taking a breath, I concentrated harder. *Come on, Rae, where are you.* I forced myself to listen past the sound of the burning building. Squeezing me lids closer together, I concentrated harder.

Then I heard it.

Coughing.

She's alive. I was so tempted to pull the mask from me face so I could better hear from which direction the sound came. I heard it again, stronger this time. Immediately I set off, the sound getting louder with each step I took.

Turning left, I entered another room and just about lost it. There in the corner was Rae, covered in soot, hugging an elderly man close. I almost tripped over me feet trying to get to her. When those big, blue eyes filled with fear latched onto me, I felt mine sting with tears of relief.

I yanked the mask off and covered her mouth with it before turning me attention to the older man. He was out cold, but still breathing. When it looked like she could take a breath without coughing, I placed the mask on the man. "I found them," I said into me radio. "I found them both, I need help getting them out." I rattled off me location before I took Rae's face in me hands.

"Can you walk?" Rae started to cough again. I knew we had to get out of there fast, me chest was starting to burn from the smoke. I hauled Mr. Bishop over me shoulder and gripped Rae's arm. She winced. That was when I saw the nasty burn on her shoulder and upper arm.

I put me arm around her waist and held her tight to me as we started the journey back. Squinting, I did me best to navigate through the thick blanket of smoke. Behind us another beam crashed to the ground, startling Rae. Me grip tightened, tugging her closer.

Heat filled me chest and me own breathing became labored. I wanted to stop and rest, but I needed to push forward. Me feet felt like lead, every step an effort. Just when reaching the end seemed impossible a figure moved through the smoke.

The moment Nathan reached us, I handed over Mr. Bishop—there was no way I was letting Rae go. I bent me knees and swept her into me arms, heading for the exit with renewed energy. I only stopped moving when I reached the waiting ambulance.

I took Rae's hand in mine and held it tight while the EMTs started working on her. Outside in the light of day that burn on her shoulder and arm looked even worse, it also reminded me how close I came to losing her.

A firm hand clasped me shoulder and squeezed hard. When I looked, Chief Abbott was behind me. He did not look happy. "You ignored a direct order."

"I know, sir." Me gaze skittered back to Rae. The oxygen mask covered half of her face and her eyes were wide. Her tears ran a line through the soot and dirt glued to her skin. Me heart couldn't take it. Biting on me teeth, I gave the chief me attention again. "I'll accept whatever reprimand comes me way."

Chief Abbott looked from me to Rae and then back at me again. "Not today, son." He smacked me shoulder and gave Rae's leg a gentle squeeze before he walked off to deal with a few reporters.

In me peripheral vision I spotted another figure coming toward us.

"Is she okay?" Thatcher rushed to the gurney, immediately looking his sister up and down. I couldn't help but glare at him. Until he turned his gaze on me. Everything I wanted to accuse him of died on me tongue when I saw the same panic and fear in his eyes I felt in me bones.

I understood why he did what he did and no amount of I-told-you-so and what-the-hell-were-you-thinking was going to change the situation. When your heart was involved, rational thinking and your ability to follow orders dissipated.

I could hardly fault the guy when I did the exact same thing.

"She needs to go to the hospital," the EMT announced.

"I'm going too." Thatcher and I said at the same time.

The EMT's gaze flitted between us before he stated, "There's just space for one of you."

I looked at Thatcher, begging him with me eyes to let me be the one to accompany Rae to the hospital. I didn't want to leave her side. I couldn't.

I held me breath as he shifted his focus to our connected hands, brows pinching.

"I'll meet you there." His voice was quiet.

A sigh of relief blew over me lips. "Thank you."

I saw Thatcher work down a swallow, his eyes glistening. "No." He shook his head. "Thank you for getting her out." With that, he spun around and stalked off.

I held onto Rae as the EMT pushed the gurney into the back of the ambulance. We'd barely pulled away from the scene when she reached up and indicated for the mask to be removed. The EMT hesitated but ultimately decided it was okay.

"You… saved… me…" her voice was soft and raspy.

Inside me chest, me heart squeezed, and I gripped her hand tighter. "It may look it, but you, *acushla*, are the one who saved me."

***

"How is she doing?"

Lifting me head from where I was cradling it in me hands, I looked in the direction of the voice. With exhaustion written all over his features, Thatcher stood in the doorway of Rae's hospital room. His gaze fixed on his sister's sleeping form. After she'd been assessed and treated, the doctor gave her something for the pain which knocked her out almost immediately.

"Considering—" Me voice sounded hoarse and raspy. I cleared me throat before I tried again. "Considering everything that's happened; she's doing good." She was incredibly lucky that the wound on her arm and shoulder was the worst of it.

Turning me attention back to the woman asleep on the bed, I brushed me fingers over hers. Me gut wrenched when, yet again, I thought about how close I came to losing her.

"No thanks to me," Thatcher mumbled as I heard him shuffle closer. The instant he reached the bed, he placed a hand on Rae's ankle. "I don't know what I would have done if she—"

"You can't go there," I cut him off. "She's safe, that's all that matters."

Out of the corner of me eye, I saw him shake his head. "Sometimes I just act without thinking. Without weighing the consequences."

Pushing to me feet, I walked over to Thatcher and placed me hand on his arm. Squeezing once, I repeated, "She's safe, man. That's all that matters."

He took his eyes off the woman we both cared about to give me a sideways glance. "You disobeyed orders, too." When I removed me hand from his arm to tuck it into me pocket, he added, "She means a lot to you."

"Aye, she does."

His gaze skittered back to Rae before he aimed a serious stare me way. "Thank you." He nodded once and then spun around to stalk out of the room. Once he was gone, I collapsed into the chair beside Rae's bed. Hanging me head, I let out a long, slow breath. Even though I'd told Thatcher not to dwell on it, I couldn't stop thinking about the day's events. About how your entire life can change in the blink of an eye.

About how close I came to losing Rae.

About how Adam lost Angie.

I realized then that it didn't matter how many times we claimed to understand someone else's pain, we really didn't know shite about it unless we've walked the same path they have.

It also dawned on me that Adam might never recover from this. Because I knew in me heart if something had happened to Rae me life would've been over.

"Gri... Griff."

The sound of her groggy voice caused me head to snap up. When I found those blue eyes of hers trained on me, I jumped up. One hand brushed the hair from her face while the other pressed the call button. "Shh, don't talk."

Lifting her arm, she touched her trembling fingers to me cheek. "You… You're… here."

I lowered me head until our foreheads touched. "And I'm not going anywhere."

EPILOGUE

RAELYN

One year later.

Grinning, I took a plate off the top of the stack, rinsed it and carefully placed it inside the dishwasher before doing the same with six other plates.

Thatcher, Brie, Lacy, Nathan, and George had left a while ago and as much as I loved our almost weekly dinner dates, I was more than happy to have Griffin all to myself.

Because, yes, even after a year of crazy monkey sex, I still couldn't get enough. Didn't think I ever would.

After I slid the last plate into its spot, I cast a glance at Griffin's closed office door. He'd slipped in there a few minutes ago to take an important call and not knowing how it was going was tightening the knots in my stomach.

Needing to keep my hands busy, I started working on the glasses and cutlery. Rinsing and loading them into the dishwasher too. I'd just stuck the last glass under the running water when I felt Griffin behind me.

His arms went around my waist, his chin resting on my shoulder. "How did it go?" I asked cautiously.

"Well, I think." Griffin took a deep breath, his chest expanding and brushing against my back. "Adam has got a long way to go still but at least he's not shutting us all out completely. Not that he's letting us in either."

About four months ago, Mrs. Carlisle had phoned us in a fit of tears. I'll be honest, I'd expected the worst when I heard her hysterics. But it was the opposite actually. Adam was finally allowing some help.

He didn't want people there every day, but he'd agreed to let his parents visit him once every two weeks. And he'd asked to see Griffin. I didn't know what exactly when down when Griffin went to see Adam.

I never asked. All I needed to know was written on his face when he came home that night. He looked relieved. Happy. Since that first visit Griffin hadn't seen Adam again but they had talked on the phone a few times.

I was very hopeful that he'd be getting his brother back soon.

"I'm sorry I left you to clean the kitchen alone," he rasped. "I should make it up to you."

Slowly, steadily his hand skimmed up under my dress. Higher and higher. My breath hitched. "What are you doing?"

Griffin's chuckle against my skin had tiny bumps popping up all over and a delicious shiver worked its way down my spine. "If you don't know then I'm not doing a very good job, am I?"

My mouth opened but instead of words a low moan rolled off my tongue. His fingers snuck past the silky barrier of my underwear and worked my body like only he knew how.

One hand gripping my hip, his tongue slick and hot gliding over my neck. Teeth scraping skin.

My fingers curled tightly around the cold metal sink while his found a faster rhythm.

"So… good," I panted. "It feels so good."

Griffin's kisses moved from my ear down my jaw. I tilted my head, lips seeking lips. Wet and cold, his tongue found mine.

Tasting.

Claiming.

Devouring.

And when he pulled back and nibbled on my bottom lip, my entire world exploded.

Chest heaving, I barely had time to catch my breath before he spun me around and immediately set me on the table behind us. My dress bunched at my hips. He shoved his pants down his ass. And after moving my underwear out of the way, he was inside me.

Filling me.

Completing me.

Griffin's hips rocked against mine. His pace almost brutal as he pushed me higher and higher. I threw my head back, and he took the opportunity to suck on my chest like he'd been starving to do so.

Our movements became hurried, sloppy, as we chased our release like it was the only thing that mattered.

And when I toppled over the edge once again, Griffin was there with me. My name on his lips like a promise. Like a prayer.

Out of breath and looking all sorts of sinful, he pressed his forehead against mine. His fingers brushed over my cheek in an achingly soft caress. "I love you, Rae."

My lips brushed over his, once, twice. "I love you right back."

MORE WORKS

Standalone Titles:
An Inconvenient Marriage

Novellas:
The Other Brother

Fake it, for real

Willow Creek:
Shattered (Willow Creek #1)

Wrecked (Willow Creek #2)

Ruined (Willow Creek #3)

Montana Dudes:
Hearts Astray

Cocky Hero Club:
Egotistical Jerk

For more information on any of these titles and future releases please visit **www.akmacbride.com**

Printed in Great Britain
by Amazon

45987747R00108